Dear Reader,

Looking back ov... [barcode] realise that thirty of them have gone by since I wrote my first book—*Sister Peters in Amsterdam*. It wasn't until I started writing about her that I found that once I had started writing, nothing was going to make me stop—and at that time I had no intention of sending it to a publisher. It was my daughter who urged me to try my luck.

I shall never forget the thrill of having my first book accepted. A thrill I still get each time a new story is accepted. Writing to me is such a pleasure, and seeing a story unfolding on my old typewriter is like watching a film and wondering how it will end. Happily of course.

To have so many of my books re-published is such a delightful thing to happen and I can only hope that those who read them will share my pleasure in seeing them on the bookshelves again...and enjoy reading them.

Betty Neels

Back by Popular Demand

A collector's edition of favourite titles from one of the world's best-loved romance authors. Mills & Boon® are proud to bring back these sought after titles and present them as one cherished collection.

BETTY NEELS: COLLECTOR'S EDITION

THE PROPOSAL

BY
BETTY NEELS

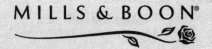

MILLS & BOON®

The Proposal *was first published in Great Britain 1993 by*
Mills & Boon Limited, and Making Sure of Sarah *was first published
in Great Britain 1999 by Mills & Boon Limited*
This edition 2001
*Harlequin Mills & Boon Limited,
Eton House, 18-24 Paradise Road, Richmond, Surrey TW9 1SR*

THE PROPOSAL © Betty Neels 1993
MAKING SURE OF SARAH © Betty Neels 1999

ISBN 0 263 82837 9

73-1101

*Printed and bound in Spain
by Litografia Rosés S.A., Barcelona*

CHAPTER ONE

THE HAZY early morning sun of September had very little warmth as yet, but it turned the trees and shrubs of the park to a tawny gold, encouraging the birds to sing too, so that even in the heart of London there was an illusion of the countryside.

The Green Park was almost empty so early in the day; indeed the only person visible was a girl, walking a Yorkshire terrier on a long lead. She was a tall girl with a tawny mane of hair and vivid blue eyes set in a pretty face, rather shabbily dressed; although her clothes were well cut they were not in the height of fashion.

She glanced at her watch; she had walked rather further than usual so Lady Mortimor, although she wouldn't be out of bed herself, would be sure to enquire of her maid if the early morning walk with Bobo had taken the exact time allowed for it. She could have walked for hours... She was on the point of turning on her heel when something large, heavy and furry cannoned into her from the back and she sat down suddenly and in a most unladylike fashion in a tangle of large dog, a hysterical Bobo and Bobo's lead. The dog put an enormous paw on her chest and grinned happily down at her before licking her cheek gently and then turning his attention to Bobo; possibly out of friendliness he kept his paw on her chest, which made getting to her feet a bit of a problem.

A problem solved by the arrival of the dog's owner—it had to be its owner, she decided…only a giant could control a beast of such size and this man, from her horizontal position, justified the thought; he was indeed large, dressed in trousers and a pullover and, even from upside-down, handsome. What was more, he was smiling…

He heaved her to her feet with one hand and began to dust her down. 'I do apologise,' he told her in a deep, rather slow voice. 'Brontes has a liking for very small dogs…'

The voice had been grave, but the smile tugging at the corners of his thin mouth annoyed her. 'If you aren't able to control your dog you should keep him on a lead,' she told him tartly, and then in sudden fright, 'Where's Bobo? If he's lost, I'll never—'

'Keep calm,' begged the man in a soothing voice which set her teeth on edge, and whistled. His dog bounded out from the bushes near by and his master said, 'Fetch,' without raising his voice and the animal bounded off again to reappear again very shortly with Bobo's lead between his teeth and Bobo trotting obediently at the other end of it.

'Good dog,' said the man quietly. 'Well, we must be on our way. You are quite sure you are not hurt?' He added kindly, 'It is often hard to tell when one is angry as well.'

'I am not angry, nor am I hurt. It was lucky for you that I wasn't an elderly dowager with a Peke.'

'Extremely lucky. Miss…?' He smiled again, studying her still cross face from under heavy lids. 'Renier Pitt-Colwyn.' He offered a hand and engulfed hers in a firm grasp.

'Francesca Haley. I—I have to go.' Curiosity got the better of good sense. 'Your dog—that's a strange name?'

'He has one eye….'

'Oh, one of the Cyclopes. Goodbye.'

'Goodbye, Miss Haley.' He stood watching her walking away towards the Piccadilly entrance to the park. She didn't look back, and presently she broke into an easy run and, when Bobo's little legs could no longer keep up, scooped him into her arms and ran harder as far as the gate. Here she put him down and walked briskly across the road into Berkeley Street, turned into one of the elegant, narrow side-streets and went down the area steps of one of the fine houses. One of Lady Mortimor's strict rules was that she and Bobo should use the tradesmen's entrance when going for their thrice-daily outings. The magnificent entrance hall was not to be sullied by dirty paws, or for that matter Francesca's dirty shoes.

The door opened onto a dark passage with white-washed walls and a worn lino on the floor; it smelled of damp, raincoats, dog and a trace of cooked food, and after the freshness of the early morning air in the park it caused Francesca's nose to wrinkle. She opened one of the doors in the passage, hung up the lead, dried Bobo's paws and went through to the kitchen.

Lady Mortimor's breakfast tray was being prepared

and her maid, Ethel, was standing by the table, squeezing orange juice. She was an angular woman with eyes set too close together in a mean face, and she glanced at the clock as Francesca went in, Bobo under one arm. Francesca, with a few minutes to spare, wished her good morning, adding cheerfully, 'Let Lady Mortimor know that Bobo has had a good run, will you, Ethel? I'm going over for my breakfast; I'll be back as usual.' She put the little dog down and the woman nodded surlily. Bobo always went to his mistress's room with her breakfast tray and that meant that Francesca had almost an hour to herself before she would begin her duties as secretary-companion to that lady. A title which hardly fitted the manifold odd jobs which filled her day.

She went back out of the side-door and round to the back of the house, past the elegant little garden to the gate which led to the mews behind the terrace of houses. Over the garage she had her rooms, rather grandly called by Lady Mortimor a flat, where she and her young sister lived. The flat was the reason for her taking the job in the first place, and she was intent on keeping it, for it made a home for the pair of them and, although Lady Mortimor made it an excuse for paying her a very small salary, at least they had a roof over their heads.

Lucy was up and dressed and getting their breakfast. She was very like her sister, although her hair was carroty instead of tawny and her nose turned up. Later on, in a few years' time, she would be as pretty as Francesca, although at fourteen she anguished over her appearance, her ambition being to grow up as quickly as possible, marry a very rich man and live in great comfort with Francesca sharing her home. An arrangement, Francesca had pointed out, which might not suit her husband. 'I hate you working for that horrid old woman,' Lucy had said fiercely.

'Well, love,' Francesca had been matter-of-fact about it, 'it's a job and we have a home of sorts and you're being educated. Only a few more years and you will have finished school and embarked on a career which will astonish the world and I shall retire.'

Now she took off her cardigan and set about laying the table in the small sitting-room with its minute alcove which housed the cooking stove and the sink.

'I had an adventure,' she said to her sister, and over the boiled eggs told her about it.

'What kind of a dog?' Lucy wanted to know.

'Well, hard to tell—he looked like a very large St Bernard from the front, but he sort of tapered off towards the tail, and that was long enough for two dogs. He was very obedient.'

'Was the man nice to him?' asked Lucy anxiously, having a soft spot for animals; indeed, at that very moment there was a stray mother cat and kittens living clandestinely in a big box under the table.

'Yes—he didn't shout and the dog looked happy. It had one eye—I didn't have time to ask why. It had a funny name, too—Brontes—that's—'

'I know—one of the Cyclopes. Could you meet the man again and ask?'

Francesca thought about it. 'Well, no, not really…'

'Was he a nice man?'

'I suppose so.' She frowned. 'He thought it was funny, me falling over.'

'I expect it was,' said Lucy. 'I'd better go or I'll miss the bus.'

After Lucy had gone she cleared away the breakfast things, tidied the room and their bedroom, and made sure that she herself was tidy too, and then she went back to the house. She was expected to lunch off a tray at midday and she seldom got back until six o'clock each evening; she arranged food for the cat, made sure that the kittens were alive and well, and locked the door.

Her employer was still in bed, sitting up against lacy pillows, reading her letters. In her youth Lady Mortimor had been a handsome woman; now in her fifties, she spent a good part of her days struggling to retain her looks. A face-lift had helped; so had the expert services of one of the best hairdressers in London and the daily massage sessions and the strict diet, but they couldn't erase the lines of discontent and petulance.

Francesca said good morning and stood listening to the woman's high-pitched voice complaining of lack of sleep, the incompetence of servants and the tiresome bills which had come in the post. When she had finished Francesca said, as she nearly always did, 'Shall I attend to the bills first, Lady Mortimor, and write the cheques and leave them for you to sign? Are there any invitations you wish me to reply to?'

Lady Mortimor tossed the pile of letters at her. 'Oh, take the lot and endeavour to deal with them—is there anything that I should know about this morning?'

'The household wages,' began Francesca, and flushed at Lady Mortimor's snide,

'Oh, to be sure you won't forget those…'

'Dr Kennedy is coming to see you at eleven o'clock. Will you see him in the morning-room?'

'Yes, I suppose so; he really must do something about my palpitations—what else?'

'A fitting for two evening gowns at Estelle, lunch with Mrs Felliton.'

'While I am lunching you can get my social diary up to date, do the flowers for the dining-room, and go along to the dry-cleaners for my suit. There will be some letters to type before you go, so don't idle away your time. Now send Ethel to me, have the cheques and wages book ready for me by half-past ten in the morning-room.' As Francesca went to the door she added, 'And don't forget little Bobo…'

'Thank you or please would be nice to hear from time to time,' muttered Francesca as she went to get the wages book, a weekly task which at least gave her the satisfaction of paying herself as well as the rest of the staff. She entered the amounts, got out the cash box from the wall safe and put it ready for Lady Mortimor, who liked to play Lady Bountiful on Fridays and pay everyone in cash. The bills took longer; she hadn't quite finished them when Maisie, the housemaid, brought her a cup of coffee. She got on well with the staff—with the exception of Ethel, of course; once they saw that she had no intention of encroaching on their ground, and was a lady to boot, with a quiet voice and manner, they accepted her for what she was.

Lady Mortimor came presently, signed the cheques, handed out the wages with the graciousness of royalty bestowing a favour and, fortified with a tray of coffee, received Dr Kennedy, which left Francesca free to tidy the muddled desk she had left behind her and take Bobo for his midday walk, a brisk twenty minutes or so before she went back to eat her lunch off a tray in the now deserted morning-room. Since the lady of the house was absent, Cook sent up what Maisie described as a nice little bit of hake with parsley sauce, and a good, wholesome baked custard to follow.

Francesca ate the lot, drank the strong tea which went with it and got ready to go to the cleaners. It wasn't far; Lady Mortimor patronised a small shop in Old Bond Street and the walk was a pleasant one. The day had turned out fine as the early morning had indicated it might and she allowed her thoughts to roam, remembering wistfully the pleasant house in Hampstead Village where they had lived when her parents had been alive. That had been four years ago now; she winced at the memory of discovering that the house had been mortgaged and the debts so large that they had swallowed up almost all the money there was. The only consolation had been the trust set aside for Lucy's education so that she had been able to stay on as a day pupil at the same well-known school.

There had been other jobs of course, after learning typing and shorthand at night-school while they lived precariously with her mother's elderly housekeeper, but she had known that she would have to find a home of their own as quickly as possible. Two years ago she had answered Lady Mortimor's advertisement and since it offered a roof over their heads and there was no objection to Lucy, provided she never entered the house, she had accepted it, aware that her wages were rather less than Maisie's and knowing that she could never ask for a rise: Lady Mortimor would point out her free rooms and all the advantages of working in a well-run household and the pleasant work.

All of which sounded all right but in practice added up to ten hours a day of taking orders with Sundays free. Well, she was going to stay until Lucy had finished school—another four years. I'll be almost thirty, thought Francesca gloomily, hurrying back with the suit; there were still the flowers to arrange and the diary to bring up to date, not to mention the letters and a last walk for Bobo.

It was pouring with rain the next morning, but that didn't stop Bobo, in a scarlet plastic coat, and Francesca, in a well-worn Burberry, now in its tenth year, going for their morning walk. With a scarf tied over her head, she left Lucy getting dressed, and led the reluctant little dog across Piccadilly and into the Green Park. Being Saturday morning, there were very few people about, only milkmen and postmen and some over-enthusiastic joggers. She always went the same way for if by any evil chance Bobo should run away and get lost, he had more chance of staying around a part of the park with which he was familiar. The park was even emptier than the streets and, even if Francesca had allowed herself to hope that she might meet the man and his great dog, common sense told her that no one in their right mind would do more than give a dog a quick walk through neighbouring streets.

They were halfway across the park, on the point of turning back, when she heard the beast's joyful barking and a moment later he came bounding up. She had prudently planted her feet firmly this time but he stopped beside her, wagging his long tail and gently nuzzling Bobo before butting her sleeve with his wet head, his one eye gleaming with friendliness.

His master's good-morning was genial. 'Oh, hello,' said Francesca. 'I didn't expect you to be here—the weather's so awful.'

A remark she instantly wished unsaid; it sounded as though she had hoped to meet him. She went pink and looked away from him and didn't see his smile.

'Ah—but we are devoted dog owners, are we not?' he asked easily. 'And this is a good place for them to run freely.'

'I don't own Bobo,' said Francesca, at pains not to mislead him. 'He belongs to Lady Mortimor; I'm her companion.'

He said, half laughing, 'You don't look in the least like a companion; are they not ladies who find library books and knitting and read aloud? Surely a dying race.'

If he only knew, she thought, but all she said cheerfully was, 'Oh, it's not as bad as all that, and I like walking here with Bobo. I must go.'

She smiled at him from her pretty, sopping-wet face. 'Goodbye, Mr Pitt-Colwyn.'

'*Tot ziens,* Miss Francesca Haley.'

She bent to pat Brontes. 'I wonder why he has only one eye?' she said to herself more than to him, and then walked briskly away, with Bobo walking backwards in an effort to return to his friend. Hurrying now, because she would be late back, she wondered what he had said instead of goodbye—something foreign and, now she came to think of it, he had a funny name too; it had sounded like Rainer, but she wasn't sure any more.

It took her quite a while to dry Bobo when they got back, and Ethel, on the point of carrying Lady Mortimor's tray upstairs, looked at the kitchen clock in triumph.

Francesca saw the look. 'Tell Lady Mortimor that I'm late back, by all means,' she said in a cool voice. 'You can tell her too that we stayed out for exactly the right time but, unless she wishes Bobo to spoil everything in her bedroom, he needs to be thoroughly dried. It is raining hard.'

Ethel sent her a look of dislike and Cook, watching from her stove, said comfortably, 'There's a nice hot cup of tea for you, Miss Haley; you drink it up before you go to your breakfast. I'm sure none of us wants to go out in such weather.'

Ethel flounced away, Bobo at her heels, and Francesca drank her tea while Cook repeated all the more lurid news from the more sensational Press. 'Don't you take any notice of that Ethel, likes upsetting people, she does.'

Francesca finished her tea. 'Well, she doesn't need to think she'll bother me, Cook, and thanks for the tea, it was lovely.'

Lucy would be home at midday since it was Saturday, and they made the shopping list together since she was the one who had to do it.

'Did you see him again?' asked Lucy.

'Who?' Francesca was counting out the housekeeping money. 'The man and his great dog? Yes, but just to say good morning.' She glanced up at her sister. 'Do you suppose I should go another way round the park? I mean, it might look as though I was wanting to meet him.'

'Well don't you?'

'He laughs at me—oh, not out loud, but behind his face.'

'I shall come with you tomorrow and see him for myself.'

On Sundays Francesca took Bobo for his morning run before being allowed the rest of the day free. 'He's not likely to be there so early on a Sunday…'

'All the same, I'll come. What shall we do tomorrow? Could we go to Regent Street and look at the shops? And have something at McDonald's?'

'All right, love. You need a winter coat…'

'So do you. Perhaps we'll find a diamond ring or a string of pearls and get a reward.'

Francesca laughed. 'The moon could turn to cheese. My coat is good for another winter—I've stopped growing but you haven't. We'll have a good look around and when I've saved enough we'll buy you a coat.'

Lady Mortimor had friends to lunch which meant that Francesca had to do the flowers again and then

hover discreetly in case her employer needed anything.

'You may pour the drinks,' said Lady Mortimor
graciously, when the guests had settled themselves in
the drawing-room, and then in a sharp aside, 'And
make sure that everyone gets what she wants.'

So Francesca went to and fro with sherry and gin
and tonic and, for two of the ladies, whisky. Cool and
polite, aware of being watched by critical eyes, and
disliking Lady Mortimor very much for making her
do something which Crow the butler should be doing.
Her employer had insisted that when she had guests
for lunch it should be Francesca who saw to the
drinks; it was one of the spiteful gestures she made
from time to time in order, Francesca guessed, to keep
her in her place. Fortunately Crow was nice about it;
he had a poor opinion of his mistress, the widow of
a wholesale textile manufacturer who had given away
enough money to be knighted, and he knew a lady
born and bred when he saw Francesca, as he informed
Cook.

When the guests had gone, Lady Mortimor went
out herself. 'Be sure and have those letters ready for
me—I shall be back in time to dress,' she told Francesca. 'And be sure and make a note in the diary—
Dr Kennedy is bringing a specialist to see me on
Tuesday morning at ten o'clock. You will stay with
me of course—I shall probably feel poorly.'

Francesca thought that would be very likely. Eating
too much rich food and drinking a little too much as
well... She hoped the specialist would prescribe a
strict diet, although on second thoughts that might not

do—Lady Mortimor's uncertain temper might become even more uncertain.

Sundays were wonderful days; once Bobo had been taken for his walk she was free, and even the walk was fun for Lucy went with her and they could talk. The little dog handed over to a grumpy Ethel, they had their breakfast and went out, to spend the rest of the morning and a good deal of the afternoon looking at the shops, choosing what they would buy if they had the money, eating sparingly at McDonald's and walking back in the late afternoon to tea in the little sitting-room and an evening by the gas fire with the cat and kittens in their box between them.

Monday always came too soon and this time there was no Brontes to be seen, although the morning was fine. Francesca went back to the house to find Lady Mortimor in a bad temper so that by the end of the day she wanted above all things to rush out of the house and never go back again. Her ears rang with her employer's orders for the next day. She was to be earlier than usual—if Lady Mortimor was to be ready to be seen by the specialist then she would need to get up earlier than usual, which meant that the entire household would have to get up earlier too. Francesca, getting sleepily from her bed, wished the man to Jericho.

Lady Mortimor set the scene with all the expertise of a stage manager; she had been dressed in a velvet housecoat over gossamer undies, Ethel had arranged her hair in artless curls and tied a ribbon in them, and she had made up carefully with a pale foundation. She had decided against being examined in her bedroom;

the *chaise-longue* in the dressing-room adjoining would be both appropriate and convenient. By half-past nine she was lying, swathed in shawls, in an attitude of resigned long-suffering.

There was no question of morning coffee, of course, and that meant that Francesca didn't get any either. She was kept busy fetching the aids Lady Mortimor considered vital to an invalid's comfort: eau-de-Cologne, smelling salts, a glass of water...

'Mind you pay attention,' said that lady. 'I shall need assistance from time to time and probably the specialist will require things held or fetched.'

Francesca occupied herself wondering what these things might be. Lady Mortimor kept talking about a specialist, but a specialist in what? She ventured to ask and had her head bitten off with, 'A heart consultant of course, who else? The best there is—I've never been one to grudge the best in illness...'

Francesca remembered Maisie and her scalded hand a few months previously. Lady Mortimor had dismissed the affair with a wave of the hand and told her to go to Out-patients during the hour she had off each afternoon. Her tongue, itching to give voice to her strong feelings, had to be held firmly between her teeth.

Ten o'clock came, with no sign of Dr Kennedy and his renowned colleague, and Lady Mortimor, rearranging herself once again, gave vent to a vexed tirade. 'And you, you stupid girl, might have had the sense to check with the consulting-rooms to make sure that this man has the time right. Really, you are completely useless...'

Francesca didn't say a word; she had lost her breath
for the moment, for the door had opened and Dr Kennedy followed by Mr Pitt-Colwyn were standing
there. They would have heard Lady Mortimor, she
thought miserably, and would have labelled her as a
useless female at everyone's beck and call.

'Well, can't you say something?' asked Lady Mortimor and at the same time became aware of the two
men coming towards her, so that her cross face became all charm and smiles and her sharp voice soft-
ened to a gentle, 'Dr Kennedy, how good of you to
come. Francesca, my dear, do go and see if Crow is
bringing the coffee—'

'No coffee, thank you,' said Dr Kennedy. 'Here is
Professor Pitt-Colwyn, Lady Mortimor. You insisted
on the best heart specialist, and I have brought him
to see you.'

Lady Mortimor put out a languid hand. 'Professor—how very kind of you to spare the time to see
me. I'm sure you must be a very busy man.'

He hadn't looked at Francesca; now he said with
grave courtesy, 'Yes, I am a busy man, Lady Mortimor.' He pulled up a chair and sat down. 'If you will
tell me what is the trouble?'

'Oh, dear, it is so hard to begin—I have suffered
poor health every day since my dear husband died. It
is hard to be left alone at my age—with so much life
ahead of me.' She waved a weak hand. 'I suffer from
palpitations, Professor, really alarmingly so; I am convinced that I have a weak heart. Dr Kennedy assures
me that I am mistaken, but you know what family

doctors are, only too anxious to reassure one if one is suffering from some serious condition...'

Professor Pitt-Colwyn hadn't spoken, there was no expression upon his handsome face and Francesca, watching from her discreet corner, thought that he had no intention of speaking, not at the moment at any rate. He allowed his patient to ramble on in a faint voice, still saying nothing when she paused to say in a quite different tone, 'Get me some water, Francesca, can't you see that I am feeling faint? And hurry up, girl.'

The glass of water was within inches of her hand. Francesca handed it, quelling a powerful desire to pour its contents all over Lady Mortimor's massive bosom.

She went back to her corner from where she admired the professor's beautiful tailored dark grey suit. He had a nice head too, excellent hair—she considered the sprinkling of grey in it was distinguished—and he had nice hands. She became lost in her thoughts until her employer's voice, raised in barely suppressed temper, brought her back to her surroundings.

'My smelling salts—I pay you to look after me, not stand there daydreaming—' She remembered suddenly that she had an audience and added in a quite different voice, 'Do forgive me—I become so upset when I have one of these turns, I hardly know what I'm saying.'

Neither man answered. Francesca administered the smelling salts and the professor got to his feet. 'I will take a look at your chest, Lady Mortimor,' and he stood aside while Francesca removed the shawls and the housecoat and laid a small rug discreetly over the patient's person.

The professor had drawn up a chair, adjusted his stethoscope and begun his examination. He was very thorough and when he had done what was necessary he took her blood-pressure, sat with Lady Mortimor's hand in his, his fingers on her pulse.

Finally he asked, 'What is your weight?'

Lady Mortimor's pale make-up turned pink. 'Well, really I'm not sure…' She looked at Francesca, who said nothing, although she could have pointed out that within the last few months a great many garments had been let out at the seams…

'You are overweight,' said the professor in measured tones, 'and that is the sole cause of your palpitations. You should lose at least two stone within the next six months, take plenty of exercise—regular walking is to be recommended—and small light meals and only moderate drinking. You will feel and look a different woman within that time, Lady Mortimor.'

'But my heart—'

'It is as sound as a bell; I can assure you that there is nothing wrong with you other than being overweight.'

He got up and shook her hand. 'If I may have a word with Dr Kennedy—perhaps this young lady can show us somewhere we can be private.'

'You are hiding something from me,' declared Lady Mortimor. 'I am convinced that you are not telling me the whole truth.'

His eyes were cold. 'I am not in the habit of lying, Lady Mortimor; I merely wish to discuss your diet with Dr Kennedy.'

Francesca had the door open and he went past her, followed by Dr Kennedy. 'The morning-room,' she told them. 'There won't be anyone there at this time in the morning.'

She led the way and ushered them inside. 'Would you like coffee?'

The professor glanced at his companion and politely declined, with a courteous uninterest which made her wonder if she had dreamed their meetings in the park. There was no reason why he shouldn't have made some acknowledgement of them—not in front of Lady Mortimor, of course. Perhaps now he had seen her here he had no further interest; he was, she gathered, an important man in his own sphere.

She went back to Lady Mortimor and endured that lady's peevish ill humour for the rest of the day. The next day would be even worse, for by then Dr Kennedy would have worked out a diet.

Of course, she told Lucy when at last she was free to go to her rooms.

'I say, what fun—was he pompous?'

'No, not in the least; you couldn't tell what he was thinking.'

'Oh, well, doctors are always poker-faced. He might have said hello.'

Francesca said crossly, 'Why should he? We haven't anything in common.' She added a little sadly, 'Only I thought he was rather nice.'

Lucy hugged her. 'Never mind, Fran, I'll find you

a rich millionaire who'll adore you forever and you'll marry him and live happily ever after.'

Francesca laughed. 'Oh, what rubbish. Let's get the washing-up done.'

As she set out with Bobo the next morning, she wished that she could have taken a different route and gone at a different time, but Lady Mortimor, easy-going when it came to her own activities and indifferent as to whether they disrupted her household, prided herself on discipline among her staff; she explained this to her circle of friends as caring for their welfare, but what it actually meant was that they lived by a strict timetable and since, with the exception of Francesca, she paid them well and Cook saw to it that the food in the kitchen was good and plentiful, they abided by it. It was irksome to Francesca and she was aware that Lady Mortimor knew that; she also knew that she and Lucy needed a home and that not many people were prepared to offer one.

So Francesca wasn't surprised to see Brontes bounding to meet her, followed in a leisurely manner by his master. She was prepared for it, of course; as he drew level she wished him a cold good-morning and went on walking, towing Bobo and rather hampered by Brontes bouncing to and fro, intent on being friendly.

Professor Pitt-Colywn kept pace with her. 'Before you go off in high dudgeon, be good enough to listen to me.' He sounded courteous; he also sounded as though he was in the habit of being listened to if he wished.

'Why?' asked Francesca.

'Don't be silly. You're bristling with indignation because I ignored you yesterday. Understandable, but typical of the female mind. No logic. Supposing I had come into the room exclaiming, "Ah, Miss Francesca Haley, how delightful to meet you again"—and it was delightful, of course—how would your employer have reacted?' He glanced at her thoughtful face. 'Yes, exactly, I have no need to dot the *I*s or cross the *T*s. Now that that slight misunderstanding is cleared up, tell me why you work for such a tiresome woman.'

She stood still the better to look at him. 'It is really none of your business…'

He brushed that aside. 'That is definitely something I will decide for myself.' He smiled down at her. 'I'm a complete stranger to you; you can say anything you like to me and I'll forget it at once if you wish me to—'

'Oh, the Hippocratic oath.'

His rather stern mouth twitched. 'And that too. You're not happy there, are you?'

She shook her head. 'No, and it's very kind of you to—to bother, but there is really nothing to be done about it.'

'No, there isn't if you refuse to tell me what is wrong.' He glanced at his watch. 'How long do you have before you have to report back?'

'Fifteen minutes.'

'A lot can be said in that time. Brontes and I will walk back with you as far as Piccadilly.'

'Oh, will you?'

'Did I not say so?' He turned her round smartly, and whistled to Brontes. 'Now consider me your favourite uncle,' he invited.

CHAPTER TWO

AFTERWARDS Francesca wondered what had possessed her. She had told Professor Pitt-Colwyn everything. She hadn't meant to, but once she got started she had seemed unable to stop. She blushed with shame just remembering it; he must have thought her a complete fool, sorry for herself, moaning on and on about her life. That this was a gross exaggeration had nothing to do with it; she would never be able to look him in the face again. The awful thing was that she would have to unless he had the decency to walk his dog in another part of the park.

She was barely in the park before he joined her.

'A splendid morning,' he said cheerfully. 'I enjoy the autumn, don't you?' He took Bobo's lead from her and unclipped it. 'Let the poor, pampered beast run free. Brontes will look after him; he has a strong paternal instinct.'

It was difficult to be stand-offish with him. 'He's a nice dog, only he's—he's rather a mixture, isn't he?'

'Oh, decidedly so. Heaven knows where he got that tail.'

For something to say, for she was feeling suddenly shy, 'He must have been a delightful puppy.'

'I found him in a small town in Greece. Someone had poked out his eye and beaten him almost to death—he was about eight weeks old.'

'Oh, the poor little beast—how old is he now?'

'Eight months old and still growing. He's a splendid fellow and strangely enough, considering his origin, very obedient.'

'I must get back.' She looked around for Bobo, who was nowhere in sight, but in answer to her companion's whistle Brontes came trotting up with Bobo scampering beside him. The professor fastened his lead and handed it to her. His goodbye was casually kind; never once, she reflected as she walked back to the house, had he uttered a word about her beastly job. She had been a great fool to blurt out all her worries and grumbles to a complete stranger who had no interest in her anyway. She wished most heartily that there was some way in which she could avoid meeting him ever again.

She thought up several schemes during the course of the day, none of which held water, and which caused her to get absent-minded so that Lady Mortimor had the pleasure of finding fault with her, insisting that she re-type several letters because the commas were in the wrong place. It was after seven o'clock by the time Francesca got back to her room over the garage and found Lucy at her homework.

'You've had a beastly day.' Lucy slammed her books shut and got out a cloth and cutlery. 'I put some potatoes in the oven to bake; they'll be ready by now. We can open a tin of beans, too. The kettle's boiling; I'll make a cup of tea.'

'Lovely, darling, I've had a tiresome day. How's school? Did you get an A for your essay?'

'Yes. Did you see him this morning?'

'Yes, just for a moment...'

'Didn't you talk at all?'

'Only about his dog.' Francesca poured them each a cup of tea and then sat down to drink it. 'I wish I'd never told him—'

'Oh, pooh—I dare say he's forgotten already. He must have lots of patients to think about; his head must be full of people's life histories.'

Francesca opened the tin of beans. 'Yes, of course, only I wish I need never see him again.'

To her secret unacknowledged chagrin, it seemed that she was to have her wish. He wasn't there the following morning, nor for the rest of the week; she told herself that it was a great relief and said so to Lucy, who said, 'Rubbish, you know you want to see him again.'

'Well—yes, perhaps. It was nice to have someone to talk to.' Francesca went on briskly, 'I wonder if it would be a good idea to go to evening classes when they start next month?'

Lucy looked at her in horror. 'Darling, you must be crazy—you mean sit for two hours learning Spanish or how to upholster a chair? I won't let you. Don't you see the kind of people who go to evening classes are very likely like us—without friends and family? Even if you got to know any of them they'd probably moan about being lonely...'

Francesca laughed. 'You know that's not quite true,' she said, 'although I do see what you mean.'

'Good. No evening classes. Doesn't Lady Mortimor have men visitors? She's always giving dinner parties…'

Francesca mentally reviewed her employer's guests; they were all past their prime. Well-to-do, self-satisfied and loud-voiced. They either ignored her in the same way as they ignored Crow or Maisie, or they made vapid remarks like, 'How are you today, little girl?' Which, since she was all of five feet ten inches tall and splendidly built, was an extremely silly thing to say.

She said, laughing, 'I can't say I've ever fancied any of them. I shall wait until you are old enough and quite grown-up, and when you've found yourself a millionaire I shall bask in your reflected glory.' She began to clear the table. 'Let's get Mum fed while the kittens are asleep—and that's another problem…'

September remained fine until the end of the month, when wind and rain tore away the last vestiges of summer. Francesca and Bobo tramped their allotted routine each morning and returned, Bobo to be fussed over once he had been dried and brushed, Francesca to hurry to her rooms, gobble breakfast and dash back again to start on the hundred and one jobs Lady Mortimor found for her to do, which were never done to that lady's satisfaction. The strict diet to which Professor Pitt-Colwyn had restricted her might be reducing her weight, but it had increased her ill humour. Francesca, supervising the making of a salad-dressing with lemon juice to accompany the thin slices of chicken which constituted her employer's lunch, wished that he had left well alone. Let the woman be as fat as butter if she wished, she reflected savagely, chopping a head of chicory while she listened to Cook detailing the menu for the dinner party that evening. A pity the professor couldn't hear that; it was dripping with calories...

Because of the dinner party the staff lunch was cold meat and potatoes in their jackets and Francesca, knowing the extra work involved in one of Lady Mortimor's large dinner parties, had hers in the kitchen and gave a hand with the preparations.

All the guests had arrived by the time she left the house that evening; Lady Mortimor, overpoweringly regal in purple velvet, had made her rearrange the flowers in the hall, polish the glasses again, much to Maisie's rage, and then go to the kitchen to make sure that Cook had remembered how to make sweet and sour sauce, which annoyed the talented woman so much that she threatened to curdle it.

'A good thing it's Sunday tomorrow,' said Francesca, eating toasted cheese while Lucy did her homework. 'And I must think of something for the kittens.' They peered at her, snug against their mother in the cardboard box, and the very idea of finding happy homes for them worried her. How was she to know if the homes were happy and what their mother would do without them?

They went to bed presently, and she dreamt of kittens and curdled sauce and Lady Mortimor in her purple, to wake unrefreshed. At least it wasn't raining, and Lucy would go with her and Bobo, and after breakfast they would go and look at the shops, have a snack somewhere and go to evensong at St Paul's.

The house was quiet as she let herself in through the side-entrance, fastened Bobo's lead and led the little dog outside to where Lucy was waiting. There was a nip in the air, but at least it wasn't raining; they set off at a good pace, crossed into the park and took the usual path. They had reached a small clump of trees where the path curved abruptly when Bobo began to bark, and a moment later Brontes came hurtling round the corner, to leap up to greet Francesca, sniff at Lucy and turn his delighted attention to Bobo, who was yapping his small head off. They had come to a halt, not wishing to be bowled over by the warmth of the big dog's attention, which gave his master ample time to join them.

'Hello—what a pleasant morning.' He sounded as though they had met recently. Francesca knew exactly how long it had been since they had last met—ten days. She bade him good-morning in a chilly voice, and when he looked at Lucy she was forced to add, 'This is my sister, Lucy. Professor Pitt-Colwyn, Lucy.'

Lucy offered a hand. 'I hoped I'd meet you one day,' she told him, 'but of course you've been away. What do you do with your dog? Does he go with you?'

'If it's possible; otherwise he stays at home and gets spoilt. You like him?'

'He's gorgeous. We've got a cat and kittens; I expect Francesca told you that—now the kittens are getting quite big we'll have to find homes for them.' She peeped at her sister's face; she looked cross. 'I'll take Bobo for a run—will Brontes come with me?'

'He'll be delighted. We'll stroll along to meet you.'

'We should be going back,' said Francesca, still very cool.

Lucy was already darting ahead and the professor appeared not to have heard her. 'I wish to talk to you, so don't be a silly girl and put on airs—'

'Well, really—' She stopped and looked up at his bland face. 'I am not putting on airs, and there is nothing for us to talk about.'

'You're very touchy—high time you left that job.' And at her indignant gasp he added, 'Just keep quiet and listen to me.'

He took her arm and began to walk after the fast retreating Lucy and the dogs. 'You would like to leave Lady Mortimor, would you not? I know of a job which might suit you. A close friend of mine died recently, leaving a widow and a small daughter. Eloise was an actress before she married—indeed, she has returned to the stage for short periods since their marriage—now she has the opportunity to go on tour with a play and is desperate to find someone to live in her house, run it for her and look after little Peggy while she is away. The tour is three or four months and then if it is successful they will go to a London theatre. You will have *carte blanche* and the services of a daily help in the house. No days off—but Peggy will be at school so that you should have a certain amount of free time. Peggy goes to a small day school, five minutes' walk from Cornel Mews—'

'That's near Lady Mortimor's—'

'Yes—don't interrupt. Eloise will come home for the very occasional weekend or day, but since the tour is largely in the north of England that isn't likely to be very often. The salary isn't bad…' He mentioned a sum which left Francesca's pretty mouth agape.

'That's—that's…just for a week? Are you sure? Lady Mortimor…I'm not properly trained.'

'You don't need to be.' He looked down his commanding nose at her. 'Will you consider it?'

'It's not permanent—and what about the cat and her kittens?'

He said smoothly, 'It will last for several months, probably longer, and you will find it easy to find another similar post once you have a good reference.'

'Lady Mortimor won't give me one.'

'I am an old friend of Eloise; I imagine that my word will carry sufficient weight. As for the cat and kittens, they may come and live in my house; Brontes will love to have them.'

'Oh, but won't your—that is, anyone mind?'

'No. I shall be seeing Eloise later; may I tell her that you are willing to go and see her?'

'I would have liked time to think about it.'

'Well, you can have ten minutes while I round up the rest of the party.'

He had gone before she could protest, walking away from her with long, easy strides.

He had said 'ten minutes' and she suspected that he had meant what he had said. It sounded a nice job and the money was far beyond her wildest expectations, and she wouldn't be at anyone's beck and call.

Prudence told her that she was probably going out of the frying pan into the fire. On the other hand, nothing venture, nothing win. When he came back presently with Lucy chattering happily and a tired Bobo and a still lively Brontes in tow, she said at once, 'All right, I'll go and see this lady if you'll give me her address. Only it will have to be in the evening.'

'Seven o'clock tomorrow evening. Mrs Vincent, two, Cornel Mews. I'll let her know. I shan't be here tomorrow; I'll see you on Tuesday. You're free for the rest of the day?'

For one delighted moment she thought he was going to suggest that they should spend it together, but all he said was, 'Goodbye,' before he started to whistle to Brontes and turned on his heel, walking with the easy air of a man who had done what he had set out to do.

Lucy tucked an arm in hers. 'Now tell me everything—why are you going to see this Mrs Vincent?'

They started to walk back and by the time they had reached the house Lucy knew all about it. They took Bobo into the kitchen and went back to their rooms to make some coffee and talk it over.

'It won't matter whether Mrs Vincent is nice or not if she's not going to be there,' observed Lucy. 'Oh, Fran, won't it be heavenly to have no one there but us—and Peggy of course—I wonder how old she is?'

'I forgot to ask...'

'All that money,' said Lucy dreamily. 'Now we can easily both get winter coats.'

'Well, I must save as much as I can. Supposing I can't find another job?'

'Never cross your bridges until you get to them,' said Lucy. 'Come on, let's go and look at the shops.'

She put the kittens back in their box with their mother.

'I'm glad they'll all have a good home,' Francesca said.

'Yes. I wonder where it is?'

'Somewhere suitable for a professor,' said Francesca snappily. It still rankled that he had taken leave of her so abruptly. There was no reason why he shouldn't, of course. He had done his good deed for the day: found help for his friend and enabled her to leave Lady Mortimor's house.

'I shall enjoy giving her my notice,' she told Lucy.

IT SEEMED AS THOUGH Monday would never end but it did, tardily, after a day of Lady Mortimor's deep displeasure vented upon anyone and anything which came within her range, due to an early morning visit to her hairdresser who had put the wrong coloured streaks in her hair. Francesca had been ordered to make another appointment immediately so that this might be remedied at once, but unfortunately the hairdresser had no cancellations. Francesca, relaying this unwelcome news, had the receiver snatched from her and listened to her employer demanding the instant dismissal of the girl who had done her hair that morning, a demand which was naturally enough refused and added to Lady Mortimor's wrath.

'Why not get Ethel to shampoo your hair and reset it?' Francesca suggested, and was told not to be so stupid, and after that there was no hope of doing anything right… She was tired and a little cross by the time she got to their rooms to find Lucy ready with a pot of tea.

'You drink that up,' she told Francesca bracingly. 'Put on that brown jacket and skirt—I know they're old, but they're elegant—and do do your face.' She glanced at the clock. 'You've twenty minutes.'

It was exactly seven o'clock when she rang the bell of the charming little cottage in Cornel Mews. Its door was a rich dark red and there were bay trees in tubs on either side of it, and its one downstairs window was curtained in ruffled white net. She crossed her fingers for luck and took a deep breath as the door was opened.

The woman standing there was small and slim and as pretty as a picture. Her dark hair was in a fashionable tangle and she wore the kind of make-up it was difficult to separate from natural colouring. She wore a loose shirt over a very narrow short skirt and high-heeled suede boots and she could have been any age between twenty and thirty. She was in fact thirty-five.

'Miss Haley—do come in, Renier has told me all about you...' She ushered Francesca into a narrow hall and opened a door into a surprisingly large living-room. 'Sit down and do have a drink while we get to know each other.'

Francesca sat, took the sherry she was offered and, since for the moment she had had no chance to say a word, she stayed silent.

'Did Renier explain?' asked Mrs Vincent. 'You know what men are, they never listen.'

It was time she said something, thought Francesca. 'He told me that you were going on tour and needed someone to look after your daughter and keep house for you.'

'Bless the darling, he had it right.' Mrs Vincent curled up in a vast armchair with her drink. 'It's just the details—'

'You don't know anything about me,' protested Francesca.

'Oh, but I do, my daily woman is sister to Lady Mortimor's cook; besides, Renier said you were a sensible young woman with a sense of responsibility, and that's good enough for me. When can you come? I'm off at the end of next week.' She didn't give Francesca a chance to speak. 'Is the money all right? All the bills will go to my solicitor, who'll deal with them, and he'll send you a weekly cheque to cover household expenses and your salary. If you need advice or anything he'll deal with it.'

Francesca got a word in at last. 'Your daughter— how old is she? Can she meet me before I come? I have a sister who would have to live here with me.'

'That's fine. She's up in the nursery; I'll get her down.'

Mrs Vincent went out of the room and called up the narrow stairs, and presently a small girl came into the room. She was one of the plainest children Francesca had ever set eyes on: lank, pale hair, a long, thin face, small, dark eyes and an unhappy little mouth.

'She's six years old,' said Mrs Vincent in a detached way. 'Goes to school of course—very bright, so I've been told. Shake hands with Miss Haley,

Peggy. She's coming to stay with you while I'm away.'

The child shook hands with Francesca and Francesca kept the small paw in her own for a moment. 'I shall like coming here to live with you,' she said gently. 'I've a sister, too…' She remembered something. 'Have you a cat or a dog to look after?'

The child shook her head. Her mother answered for her. 'My last nanny wouldn't have them in the house, though it's all one to me.' She laughed. 'I'm not here long enough to mind.'

'Then could I bring a kitten with me? Perhaps you would like one of your very own to look after, Peggy?'

The child smiled for the first time; there was an endearing gap in her teeth. 'For my own?' she asked.

'If your mother will allow that.'

'Oh, let the child have a pet if she wants.' Mrs Vincent added unexpectedly, 'She takes after her father.'

A remark which made everything clear to Francesca; a lovely, fragile creature like Mrs Vincent would find this plain, silent child a handicap now that she was going back on the stage. Probably she loved her dearly, but she wasn't going to let her interfere with her career. She went pink when Mrs Vincent said, 'I've been left comfortably off, but I've no intention of dwindling into a lonely widowhood,' because she might have read her thoughts. She smiled suddenly. 'I shall wait for a decent interval and get married again.'

Francesca watched Peggy's small face; it was stony

with misery. She said quickly, 'I'll bring the kitten when I come, shall I? And you can choose a name for it—it's a little boy cat; he's black and white with yellow eyes.'

Peggy slipped a small hand into hers. 'Really? Will he live here with us?'

'Of course, for this will be his home, won't it?'

Eloise poured herself another drink. 'You have no idea what a relief this is—may I call you Francesca? Now when can we expect you?'

'References?' ventured Francesca.

'Renier says you're OK. That's good enough for me; I told you that.'

'I shall have to give a week's notice to Lady Mortimor. I can do that tomorrow.'

'Good. I can expect you in a week's time. Give me a ring and let me know what time of day you'll be coming and I'll make a point of being in. Now have you time to go round the cottage with me?'

It was a small place, but very comfortably furnished with a well-planned kitchen and, on the ground floor, the living-room and, on the floor above, two good-sized bedrooms and a smaller room with a small bathroom leading from it. 'This is the nursery,' said Mrs Vincent. 'Peggy plays here—she's got masses of toys; she's quite happy to amuse herself.'

Francesca wondered about that although she said nothing. 'How long will you be away?' she asked.

'Oh, my dear, how am I to know? The tour will last three months at least, and with luck will end up at a London theatre; if it doesn't I shall get my agent to find me something else.'

'Yes, of course. Has Peggy any grandparents or cousins who may want to visit?'

'My parents are in America; Jeff's live in Wiltshire, almost Somerset, actually. We don't see much of them.' Something in her voice stopped Francesca from asking any more questions, and presently she bade Mrs Vincent goodbye, and bent to shake Peggy's hand.

'You won't forget the kitten?'

'No, I'll bring him with me, I promise.'

Back in her little sitting-room she told Lucy everything. 'It's a dear little house, you'll love it. I think Peggy is lonely—she's withdrawn—perhaps she misses her father; I don't know how long ago he died. I promised her a kitten—the black and white one. Mrs Vincent didn't mind.'

'You don't like her much, do you?' asked Lucy shrewdly.

'Well, she's charming and friendly and easy-going, but she didn't seem very interested in Peggy. Perhaps it's hard to stay at home quietly with a small child if you've been used to theatre friends, and perhaps when her husband was alive they went out a lot.'

'It'll be better than Lady Mortimor's, anyway. We had better start packing up tomorrow, and don't forget Professor Pitt-Colwyn is going to take mother cat and the other kittens. Shall you meet him tomorrow?'

'He said he would be there.' She frowned. 'I must be careful what I say about Mrs Vincent; he said he was a close friend of her husband so I expect he is a close friend of hers as well.'

'Do you suppose she's got her eye on him?'

'Don't be vulgar, Lucy. I should think it was very likely, although for all we know he's married already.'

'You'd better ask him—'

'Indeed I will not.'

He was in the park, waiting for her when she got there the next morning with Bobo. It was a bright day with more than a hint of the coming winter's chill and Francesca, an elderly cardigan over her blouse and skirt, wished she had worn something warmer.

He wasted no time on good-mornings but said, 'You're cold; why didn't you wear something sensible? We had better walk briskly.'

He marched her off at a fine pace, with Bobo keeping up with difficulty and Brontes circling around them. 'Well? You saw Eloise Vincent? Are you going to take the job?'

'Yes, I'm going to give Lady Mortimor my notice this morning and let Mrs Vincent know when I'll be going to her.'

'You saw Peggy?'

'Yes.'

He looked down at her thoughtfully. 'And…?'

'She's a quiet little girl, isn't she? I said I would take one of our kittens there for her to look after; her mother said that I might. You will take the mother cat and the other kittens, won't you?'

'Certainly I will. When will it be convenient for me to collect them? One evening? Let me see, I'm free on Thursday after six o'clock. Where exactly do you live?'

'Well, over the garage at the back of the house.

There's a side-door; there's no knocker or bell, you just have to thump.'

'Then shall we say between six o'clock and half-past six? Have you a basket?'

'No, I'll get a cardboard box from the kitchen.'

'No need. I'll bring a basket with me. You're quite happy about this job?'

'Yes, thank you. You see, it's much more money and it will be so nice not to be…that is, it will be nice to be on our own.'

'That I can well believe. Are you scared of Lady Mortimor?'

She gave his question careful thought. 'No, not in the least, but she is sometimes rather rude if anything has annoyed her. I have longed to shout back at her but I didn't dare—she would have given me the sack.'

'Well, now you can bawl her out as much as you like, though I don't suppose you will; you've been too well brought up.'

He had spoken lightly, but when she looked at him she saw the mocking little smile. He must think her a spineless creature, dwindling into a dull spinster-hood. He had been kind, but his pity angered her. After all, she hadn't asked him for help. She said in her quiet voice, 'I have to go. Thank you for your help, and we'll have mother cat and the kittens ready for you when you come.' She gave him a stiff smile. 'Goodbye, Professor Pitt-Colwyn.'

She would contrive to be out when he called on Thursday evening, she decided as she made her way back to the house.

She couldn't have chosen a worse time in which to

give in her notice. Lady Mortimor had been to a bridge party on the previous day and lost money, something she couldn't bear to do, and over and above that her dressmaker had telephoned to say that the dress she had wanted delivered that morning was not finished. Francesca went into the room in time to hear her employer declaring that it was no concern of hers if the girl working on it was ill, the dress was to be delivered by two o'clock that afternoon. She glanced up when she saw Francesca. 'Better still, I'll send round a girl to collect it and it had better be ready.

'You heard that,' she snapped. 'That stupid woman having the cheek to say I can't have the dress today. I intend to wear it to the Smithers' drinks party this evening. You'll fetch it after lunch.'

She sat down at the little writing-table and glanced through the letters there. 'Bills,' she said peevishly. 'These tradespeople always wanting their money. You'd better see to them, I suppose, Francesca.' She got up. 'I've a hair appointment—see that they're ready for me when I get back.'

Francesca picked up the letters. 'Lady Mortimor, I wish to give you a week's notice as from today.' She laid an envelope on the desk. 'I have put it in writing.'

Lady Mortimor looked as though she had been hit on the head. Her eyes popped from her head, her mouth gaped. When she had her breath she said, 'What nonsense is this? You must be mad, girl. A cushy job and a flat of your own...I won't hear of it.'

'There's nothing you can do about it,' Francesca pointed out reasonably. 'It isn't a cushy job, it's very badly paid, and it surely isn't a flat—it's two small rooms with a minute kitchen and a shower which doesn't work half the time.'

'You'll have difficulty in getting work, I'll see to that. I'll not give you a reference.'

'That won't be necessary. I already have a job to go to and your reference won't be required.'

'Then you can go now, do you hear, you ungrateful girl?'

'Just as you say, Lady Mortimor. You will have to give me two weeks' wages, one in lieu of notice.' She watched her employer's complexion becoming alarmingly red. 'And whom shall I ask to arrange the dinner party for Saturday? And your lunch party on Sunday? Shall I let Ethel have the bills to check? And there will be the invitations for the charity tea party you are giving next week.'

Francesca paused for breath, astonished at herself. Really she had been most unpleasant and deserved to be thrown out of the house for rudeness. She realised that she wouldn't mind that in the least.

Lady Mortimor knew when she was worsted. 'You will remain until the following week.'

'Tuesday evening,' Francesca interpolated gently, ignoring the woman's glare.

'You will send an advertisement to the usual papers this morning. I require letters in the first instance; interviews can be arranged later to suit me.'

'Certainly, Lady Mortimor. Am I to state the salary?'

'No. The flat goes with the job, of course.' She swept to the door. 'It may interest you to know that you have ruined my day. Such ingratitude has cut me to the quick.'

Francesca forbore from saying that, for someone of Lady Mortimor's ample, corseted figure, the cut would have to be really deep.

Naturally a kind girl and seldom critical of other people, she felt guilty once she was alone. She had been most dreadfully rude; she felt thoroughly ashamed of herself. She had almost finished the bills when Maisie came in with her coffee.

'Cor, miss, what a lark—you going away. Mr Crow was just in the hall passing as you might say and 'eard it all. He said as 'ow you gave as good as you got and good luck to you, we all says—treated you something shameful, she 'as, and you a lady and all.'

'Why, Maisie, how very kind of you all. I'm afraid I was very rude…'

'A bit of plain speaking never 'urt no one, miss. I 'opes 'owever that 'oever takes yer place is capable of a bit of talking back.'

Francesca drank her coffee, feeling cheerful again. She wasn't going to apologise, but she would behave as she always had done, however unpleasant Lady Mortimor might choose to be.

She chose to be very unpleasant. It was a good thing that there were no signs of the professor the next morning for she might have burst into tears all over him and wallowed in self-pity, but by Thursday evening she didn't care any more and allowed Lady Mortimor's ill temper and spiteful remarks to flow over her head. Heedful of her decision, she took care not to get to the rooms until well after seven o'clock, only to find the professor sitting in comfort in the only easy-chair in the place, drinking tea from a mug while Brontes brooded in a fatherly fashion over mother cat and the kittens in their box.

'There you are,' said Lucy as Francesca went in. 'We thought you'd never come. There's still tea in the pot. But Renier's eaten all the biscuits; he didn't have time for lunch. Have you had a beastly day?'

'Well, a bit sticky. I say, isn't Brontes sweet?'

The professor had got up from his chair and pushed her gently into it, and had gone to sit on the small wooden chair which creaked under his weight. He said now, 'I shall be away for the next ten days or so; I hope you settle down with Peggy.' His hooded gaze swept over her tired face. 'It's time you had a change, and I think you will find she will be much nicer to live with than your Lady Mortimor.' He got up. 'I must be going.' He scooped the cat and kittens into the basket he had brought with him, while Lucy cuddled the other kitten on her lap. 'I'll take good care of them,' he said. He smiled at them both. *'Tot ziens.'* And when Francesca made an effort to rise he said, 'No, I'll see myself out.'

The room seemed very empty once he had gone.

CHAPTER THREE

THE WEEK SEEMED never-ending, and Lady Mortimor was determined to get the last ounce of work out of Francesca before she left. There had been several answers to the advertisement, but so far the applicants had refused the job. They had turned up their noses at the so-called flat and two of them had exploded with laughter when they had been told their salary. They were, they had pointed out, secretary-companions, not dog minders or errand girls. Lady Mortimor actually had been shaken. 'You will have to remain until someone suitable can take your place,' she had said the day before Francesca was due to leave.

'That won't be possible,' said Francesca. 'I start my new job immediately I leave here. One of the agencies might have help for you, but only on a daily or weekly basis.'

Lady Mortimor glared at her. 'I am aware of that, but I have no intention of paying the exorbitant fees they ask.' She hesitated. 'I am prepared to overlook your rudeness, Francesca. I am sure that you could arrange to go to this new job, say, in a weeks' time?'

'I am very sorry, Lady Mortimor, but that is impossible.'

She watched her employer sweep out of the room in a towering rage, and went back to making out the last of the cheques for the tradesmen.

The last day was a nightmare she refused to dwell upon. Lady Mortimor gave her not a moment to herself, and when six o'clock came declared that half the things she had told Francesca to do were still not done. Francesca listened quietly, allowing the tirade to flow over her head. 'There is nothing of importance left to do,' she pointed out. 'Whoever can come in place of me can deal with anything I've overlooked. Goodbye, Lady Mortimor.'

She closed the door quietly on her erstwhile employer's angry voice. She had a happier send-off from the staff, and Crow presented her with a potted plant from them all and wished her well. 'For we're all sure you deserve it, miss,' he said solemnly.

She went to join Lucy, and, after a meal, packed the last of their belongings. A taxi would take them the short distance to Cornel Mews in the morning.

Eloise Vincent was waiting for them when they arrived mid-morning. Peggy was at school, she told them. 'My daily woman will fetch her after lunch. I'm up to my eyes packing; I'm off this evening. I've written down all the names and addresses you might need and a phone number in case you should need me urgently, but for heaven's sake don't ring unless it's something dire.' She led the way upstairs. 'You each have a room; I'll leave you to unpack.' She glanced at the cat basket Lucy was holding. 'Is this the kitten? I dare say Peggy will like having him. There's coffee in the kitchen; help yourselves, will you? Lucy's bed is made up. I'm sorry I haven't put clean sheets on the other bed; the room's been turned out, but I had to empty cupboards and drawers—you won't mind doing it?'

She smiled charmingly and went downstairs, leaving them to inspect their new quarters. The rooms were prettily furnished and to have a room of one's own would be bliss. They unpacked and hung everything away and, with the kitten still in his basket, went downstairs. Mrs Wells, the daily cleaner, was in the kitchen. She was a pleasant-faced, middle-aged woman who poured coffee for them, found a saucer of milk for the kitten and offered to do anything to help. 'I've been here quite a while, before poor Dr Vincent died, so I know all there is to know about the place. I come in the mornings—eight o'clock—and go again after lunch,' she offered biscuits, 'though I said I'd fetch Peggy from school before I go home today.'

'Can't we do that?' asked Francesca. 'We have to get to know her, and it's a chance to see where the school is.'

'Well, now, that would be nice. It's at the end of Cornel Road, just round the corner in Sefton Park Street. Mrs Vincent hoped you wouldn't mind having a snack lunch—the fridge is well stocked and you can cook this evening. She is going out to lunch with a friend, but she'll be back by two o'clock and aims to leave around six o'clock—being fetched by car.'

Francesca thought of the questions she wanted answered before Mrs Vincent left. She put down her coffee-cup. 'Perhaps I could talk to her now?'

Eloise Vincent was in the sitting-room, sitting at her desk, a telephone book before her, the receiver in her hand. She looked up and smiled as Francesca went in. 'Settling in?' she asked. 'Mrs Wells is a fount of knowledge if you've any questions.'

'Yes. She's been most helpful. Mrs Vincent, could you spare a moment? Just to tell me what time Peggy goes to bed, if there's anything she won't eat, which friends is she allowed to play with while you are away...?'

'Oh, dear, what a lot of questions. She goes to bed about seven o'clock, I suppose. She eats her dinner at school and I've been giving her tea about five o'clock. I don't know about her friends. My husband used to take her with him when he went to see his friends; they haven't been here, although on her birthday we had a party, of course—'

'May I have the names of your doctor and dentist?'

Mrs Vincent laughed. 'Oh, get Renier if anything is worrying you. He's Peggy's godfather; he's fond of her. She's never ill, anyway. Now, you really must excuse me—Mrs Wells can tell you anything else you may want to know.'

It was obvious to Francesca that Mrs Vincent had no more time for her. She went back to the kitchen and did a thorough tour of its cupboards and shelves, went through the linen cupboard with Mrs Wells and, when Mrs Vincent had left for her lunch appointment, sat down with Mrs Wells and Lucy to eat sandwiches and drink more coffee.

Peggy came out of school at three o'clock, and both of them went to fetch her since Mrs Vincent wasn't back. The children came out in twos and threes and Peggy was one of the last, walking slowly and alone.

They went to meet her and she seemed pleased to see them, walking between them, holding their hands, answering their cheerful questions about school politely. Only when Francesca said, 'The kitten's waiting for you,' did she brighten. They spent the rest of the short walk discussing suitable names for him.

Mrs Vincent was back and there was a car before the door, which was being loaded with her luggage by a tall, middle-aged man. He said, 'Hello, Peggy,' without stopping what he was doing.

She said, 'Hello, Mr Seymour,' in a small wooden voice, all her animation gone again.

'You'd better go and say goodbye to your mother,' he told her over his shoulder. 'We're off in a few minutes.'

The three of them went inside and found Mrs Vincent in the sitting-room, making a last-minute phone call. 'Darlings,' she cried in her light, pretty voice, 'I'm going now. Come and say goodbye to your old mother, Peggy, and promise to be a good girl while I'm away. I'll send you lots of postcards and when I can I will telephone to you.' She kissed her small daughter and turned to Francesca. 'I'll be trying to keep in touch,' she said. 'I'm sure you'll do a marvellous job. Let me know how you are getting on from time to time.'

She smiled, looking so pretty and appealing that Francesca smiled back, quelling the uneasy feeling that Eloise Vincent was only too delighted to be starting her theatrical career once more and couldn't wait to get away.

She was prepared for Peggy's tears once her mother had gone, but the child's face had remained impassive. 'May I have the kitten now?' she asked, almost before they were out of sight.

She and the small creature took to each other at once. She sat happily in the sitting-room with him on her small, bony knees, talking to him and stroking his head with a small, gentle hand. 'I shall call him Tom,' she told Francesca.

'That's a nice name.'

'Daddy used to read me a story about Tom Kitten...' The small voice quavered and Francesca said quickly, 'Shall we talk about your daddy? I'd like to know all about him.'

So that was the trouble, she reflected, listening to the child's rambling description of her father and the fun they had had together. Peggy had loved him dearly and there had been no one to talk to her about him. She let the child chat on, the small face animated, and then said gently, 'What nice things you have to remember about him, Peggy, and of course he'll never go away; he'll always be there inside your head.'

'I like you,' said Peggy.

It took a few days to settle into a routine. Lucy went to school each morning and Francesca took Peggy to her school shortly afterwards, going back to make the beds and shop and wash and iron while Mrs Wells gave the house what she called a good tidy up. Tom settled down without any nonsense, aware by now that he belonged to Peggy and no one else, sitting beside her chair at meals and sleeping at the foot of her bed.

There had been no news of Mrs Vincent. Francesca wasn't sure where she was, for the promised list of the various towns the company would be appearing in hadn't turned up. It was a relief that at the end of the week there was a cheque in the post with her salary and a housekeeping allowance.

It was two days later, after they had had tea and Francesca was on the floor in the kitchen, showing Peggy how to play marbles while Tom pranced around them both, that the front doorbell was rung.

'I'll go,' called Lucy, in the sitting-room with her homework, and a moment later Professor Pitt-Colwyn's voice sent Peggy flying to the kitchen door. He caught her in his arms and kissed her soundly. 'Hello, love, I thought it was time I came to see how you were getting on...'

He watched Francesca get up off the floor and brush down her skirt. 'Marbles—am I in time for a game?' and then he added, 'Good evening, Francesca.'

She was surprised at how glad she was to see him. 'Good evening, Professor.' She scanned his face and saw that he was tired. 'Shall we go into the sitting-room? I'll make a cup of coffee while you and Peggy have a talk—she wants to show you Tom.'

He looked down at the small, earnest face staring up at him. 'A splendid idea—shall we be disturbing Lucy?'

'I've just finished,' said Lucy. 'I'll help Fran get the coffee—'

'A sandwich with it?' asked Francesca.

'That would be very nice.'

'Have you had no lunch or tea?'

'A rather busy day.' He smiled, and she could see that he wasn't going to talk about it.

She made a pot of coffee, cut a plateful of cold beef sandwiches and bore the tray into the sitting-room. Peggy was sitting on the professor's knee and Tom had curled upon her small lap. Francesca was astonished to hear the child's happy voice, talking nineteen to the dozen.

'We are talking about Peggy's father,' said the professor deliberately.

Francesca said at once, 'He must have been a marvellous dad. Peggy has told us a little about him.' She poured him a cup and gave it to him. 'You stay there, darling. Here's your milk, and take care not to spill it over your godfather's trousers.'

She passed the sandwiches too, and watched him eat the lot. 'There's a cake I made this afternoon,' she suggested.

He ate several slices of that too, listening to Peggy's chatter, knowing just when to make some remark to make her giggle. Francesca let her bedtime go by, for the little girl was really happy. It was the professor who said at last, 'It's way past your bedtime, Peggy,' and when she wound her arms round his neck he said, 'If you go to bed like the good girl you are, I'll come and take you to the zoo on Saturday afternoon.'

'Fran and Lucy too?'

'Of course. Tom can mind the house and we'll come back here and have an enormous tea.'

She slid off his knee. Kissed him goodnight then, and went to stand by Francesca's chair. 'Will we?' she asked. 'Will we, really?'

'If your godfather says so, then of course we will, and I'll make a simply enormous cake and we'll have crumpets dripping with butter.'

'Could Lucy put her to bed?' asked the professor. 'We might have a chat?'

'Of course I can.' Lucy scooped up the kitten and handed him to Peggy. 'And Fran will come and tuck you up when you're in bed.'

Peggy went happily enough, her hand in Lucy's and the kitten tucked under one arm. Francesca, suddenly shy, offered more coffee.

'Any problems?' asked the professor.

She thought before she answered. 'No, I don't think so. I should have liked to have known a bit more about Peggy before Mrs Vincent left, but there wasn't much time. Mrs Wells is a great help with things like shopping and so on. Peggy doesn't seem to have any friends…do you suppose it would be all right if I invited one or two children for tea one day? I think she is a very shy little girl.'

'She is a very unhappy little girl. She loved her father very much and she misses him; she likes to talk about him. I think that Eloise didn't understand that and the child is too small to carry so much hidden grief.' He glanced at her. 'She told me that she talks to you and Lucy about him.'

'Yes, he is still alive to her, isn't he? If you're sure that's the right thing to do?'

'Quite sure. By all means see if you can get some children round to play with her. Has she no friends at all at school?'

'Oh, one or two speak to her but she doesn't seem to have any special friends, but I'll do my best. She has masses of toys and it would be nice if she were to share them.'

'Have you heard from Eloise?'

'Me? No. She said she would be too busy rehearsing to write for a while.'

'I'm going to Cheltenham to see the opening show next week. If you think of anything you want to know about, let me know before then.'

'Thank you. She left everything beautifully organised. I expect she's a very good actress?'

He didn't answer, and she wondered uncomfortably if she had said something about Mrs Vincent which might have annoyed him. She couldn't think of anything but if he was in love with her, and she supposed that he was, he would be touchy about her. Lucy came in then.

'Peggy's bathed and in bed; she's waiting for you to say goodnight—both of you.'

The child wreathed her arms round Francesca's neck. 'I love you, Fran.'

'Thank you, darling. I love you too, and Tom of course. Now go to sleep quickly, won't you? Because he's asleep already.'

The professor was hugged in his turn, and he was reminded of his promise to take them to the zoo on

Saturday, then he was kissed goodnight. 'Now tuck me in, please, Fran.'

So she was tucked in and he stood in the little room, leaning against the wall, watching, his eyes half closed.

Back in the sitting-room he said, 'I must be off. Thanks for the coffee and sandwiches.'

'It made Peggy very happy to see you,' Francesca said. The thought that it had made her very happy too was sternly dismissed. 'You will have a good meal before you go to bed, won't you?'

He looked as though he were going to laugh. 'Indeed I will.' He smiled at Lucy and dropped a large hand on Francesca's shoulder for a moment and went away. Lucy went to the window to watch him drive away, but Francesca busied herself with the cups and saucers.

'I shall enjoy the zoo,' said Lucy.

'Yes, it should be fun; Peggy will love it. Lucy, I must do something about finding her some friends...'

'Well, gossip around when you go to get her from school. I dare say our Eloise discouraged them—children are noisy and they make a mess...'

'You're probably right, but don't call her that, dear—we might forget and say something—I mean, I think he's in love with her, don't you? He's going all the way to Cheltenham for the opening night.'

They were in the kitchen, washing up the coffee-cups.

'That doesn't mean that he's in love with her. What shall we have for supper? It's a bit late.'

The following day Francesca made a few tentative

overtures to the mothers and nannies taking the children to school. They were friendly enough, and she made a point of letting them know that Mrs Vincent had gone away for a time and that she was looking after Peggy. She said no more than that, but it was, she thought, the thin end of the wedge...

She wasn't sure, but she thought that maybe the children had been discouraged from getting friendly with Peggy, a child too shy to assert herself with the making of friends. It might take some time, but it would be nice if she could get to know a few children while her mother was away, so that by the time she got back home Peggy would have established a circle of little friends. Already the child was livelier, learning to play the games small children played, spending long hours with Francesca or Lucy rearranging the elaborate doll's house, planning new outfits for the expensive dolls she had. 'Woollies for the winter,' explained Francesca, getting knitting needles and wool and starting on miniature sweaters and cardigans.

They all went shopping the next day, and it was apparent that Peggy had never been to Woolworth's. They spent a long time there while she trotted from one counter to the other, deciding how to spend the pocket money Francesca had given her. After the rigours of Lady Mortimor's household, life was very pleasant. Francesca, going about her chores in the little house, planning meals, playing with Peggy, sitting in the evenings sewing or knitting, with Lucy doing her homework at the table, felt that life was delightful. They had a home, well, not a permanent one, but still a home for the time being—enough money, the prospect of having some new clothes and of adding to their tiny capital at the bank. She was almost content.

The professor came for them after lunch on Saturday, bundled them briskly into his car, and drove to the zoo. It was a mild autumn day, unexpected after several days of chilly rain. Francesca, in her good suit, her burnished hair gleaming in the sunshine, sat beside him in the car making polite small talk, while Lucy and Peggy in the back giggled and chattered together. The professor, who had been up most of the night with a very ill patient, allowed the happy chatter from the back seat to flow over his tired head and listened to Francesca's pretty voice, not hearing a word she said but enjoying the sound of it.

The afternoon was a success; they wandered along, stopping to look at whatever caught their eyes, with Peggy skipping between them until she caught sight of the camels, who were padding along with their burden of small children.

The professor fished some money out of his pocket and gave it to Lucy. 'You two have a ride; Francesca and I are going to rest our feet. We'll be here when you get back.'

'You make me feel very elderly—bunions and dropped arches and arthritic knees,' protested Francesca, laughing as they sat down on an empty bench.

'You, my dear girl, will never be elderly. That is an attitude of mind.' He spoke lightly, not looking at her. 'You have settled down quite happily, I hope?'

'Oh, yes, and Lucy and Peggy get on famously.'

'So I have noticed. And you, Francesca, you mother them both.'

She was vexed to feel her cheeks grow hot. She asked stiffly, 'How is Brontes? And mother cat and the kittens?'

'He has adopted them. You must come and see them. The children are at school during the day? You will be free for lunch one day? I'll give you a ring.'

'Is that an invitation?' asked Francesca frostily.

'Certainly it is. You want to come, don't you?'

She had no intention of saying so. 'I shall be very glad to see mother cat and the kittens again.'

His stern mouth twitched a little. 'I shall be there too; I hope you will be glad to see me.'

'Well, of course.' She opened her handbag and looked inside and closed it again for something to do. She would be very glad to see him again, only he mustn't be allowed to know that. He was merely being friendly, filling in his days until Eloise Vincent should return. She wished that she knew more about him; she voiced the wish without meaning to and instantly wanted it unsaid.

'You flatter me.' He told her blandly, 'Really there is nothing much to tell. I work—as most men work. Perhaps I am fortunate in liking that work.'

'Do you go to a hospital every day or have a surgery?'

'I go to several hospitals and I have consulting-rooms.'

She persisted. 'If you are a professor, do you teach the students?'

'Yes. To the best of my ability!' He added gently,

'I examine them too, and from time to time I travel. Mostly to examine students in hospitals in other countries. I have a very competent secretary and a nurse to help me—'

'I'm sorry, I've been very rude; I can't think why I asked you about your work or—or anything.' She had gone pink again and she wouldn't look at him, so that the long, curling lashes, a shade darker than her hair, lay on her cheeks. She looked quite beautiful and he studied her with pleasure, saying nothing. It was a great relief to her when Lucy and Peggy came running towards them. Caught up in the excited chatter from Peggy, she forgot the awkward moment.

They went back to the little house in the Mews presently and had their tea: fairy cakes and a gingerbread, little sandwiches and chocolate biscuits. 'It's like my birthday,' said Peggy, her small, plain face wreathed in smiles.

The professor stayed for an hour after tea, playing ludo on the floor in front of the sitting-room fire. When he got to his feet, towering over them, he observed pleasantly, 'A very nice afternoon—we must do it again some time.' He kissed his small goddaughter, put a friendly arm around Lucy's shoulders, and went to the door with Francesca.

'I'll phone you,' was all he said, 'and thanks for the tea.'

IT WAS several days later when she had a phone call. A rather prim voice enquired if she were Miss Haley and went on to ask if she would lunch with Professor Pitt-Colwyn in two days' time. 'If it wouldn't inconvenience you,' went on the voice, 'would you go to the Regent hospital at noon and ask for the professor?'

Francesca agreed. Were they going to eat at the hospital? she wondered, and what should she wear? It would have to be the brown suit again. Her winter coat was too shabby and although there was some money now Lucy needed a coat far more than she did. She would wash her hair and do her nails, she decided, and buy a new lipstick.

The Regent hospital was in the East End. It was a hideous building, heavily embellished with fancy brickwork of the Victorian era, brooding over a network of shabby streets. Francesca got off the bus opposite its entrance and presented herself at the reception desk inside the entrance hall.

The clerk appeared to know who she was, for she lifted the phone and spoke into it, and a moment later beckoned to one of the porters.

'If you would wait for a few minutes, Miss Haley, the porter will show you…'

Francesca followed the man, wishing that she hadn't come; she couldn't imagine the professor in this vast, echoing building. Probably he had forgotten that he had invited her and was deep in some highly urgent operation. Come to think of it, she didn't know if he was a surgeon or a physician. She sat down in a small room at the back of the entrance hall, facing a long corridor. It was empty and after a minute or two she was tempted to get up and go home, but all at once there were people in it, walking towards her: the professor, towering above the posse of people trying to keep up with him, a short, stout ward sister, two or three young men in short white coats, an older man in a long white coat, a tall, stern-looking woman with a pile of folders under one arm and, bringing up the rear, a worried-looking nurse carrying more folders.

The professor paused in the doorway of the room she was in, filling it entirely with his bulk. 'Ah, there you are,' he observed in a voice which suggested that she had been in hiding and he had just discovered her. 'Give me five minutes...'

He had gone and everyone else with him, jostling each other to keep up.

He reappeared not ten minutes later, elegant in a dark grey suit and a silk tie which had probably cost as much as her best shoes. They had been her best for some time now, and she hardly ever wore them for they pinched abominably.

'Kind of you to come here,' he told her breezily. 'I wasn't sure of the exact time at which I could be free. Shall we go?'

She walked beside him, out to the space reserved for consultants' cars and got into the car, easing her feet surreptitiously out of her shoes. The professor, watching out of the corner of his eye, turned a chuckle into a cough and remarked upon the weather.

He drove west, weaving his way through the small side-streets until she, quite bewildered by the one-way traffic, saw that they were in Shaftesbury Avenue. But only briefly; he turned into side-streets again and ten minutes or so later turned yet again into a narrow street, its trees bare of leaves now, the houses on ei-

ther side elegant Regency, each with a very small
garden before it, steps leading up to doorways topped
by equally elegant fanlights. The professor stopped
the car and got out to open her door. 'I thought we
might lunch at home,' he told her. 'Brontes is anxious
to see you again.'

'You live here?' asked Francesca. A silly question,
but she had been surprised; it was, she guessed, five
minutes away from Mrs Vincent's cottage.

'Yes.' He took her arm and marched her up the
steps as the door was opened by a dignified middle-
aged man in a black jacket and pin-striped trousers.

'Ah, Peak. Francesca, this is Peak, who sees that
this place runs on oiled wheels. Mrs Peak is my
housekeeper. Peak, this is Miss Haley. Show her
where she can leave her coat, will you?' He picked
up his bag. 'I'll be in the drawing-room, Francesca.'

In the charming little cloakroom concealed beneath
the curving staircase, she poked at her hair, added
more lipstick and deplored the suit; she had better
take off the jacket otherwise it might look as though
she were ready to dart out of the house again. Her
blouse wasn't new either, but it was ivory silk, laun-
dered and pressed with great care, and the belt around
her slender waist was soft leather. Her feet still hurt,
but she would be able to ease them out of her shoes
again once they were sitting at the table. She went
back into the narrow hall and the professor appeared
at a half-open door.

'Come and have a drink before lunch.' He held the
door wide and Brontes stuck his great head round it,
delighted to see her.

The room was long and narrow, with a bay window overlooking the street and a charming Adam fireplace. The chairs were large and deep and well cushioned, and there was a scattering of small lamp tables as well as a handsome bow-fronted display cabinet embellished with marquetry, its shelves filled with silver and porcelain. The professor went to the rent table under the window. He asked, 'Sherry for you? And do sit down.'

She sat, and was aware that mother cat and her kittens were cosily curled up together in one of the easy chairs. She said, 'Oh, they seem very much at home.'

He handed her the sherry. 'Brontes has seen to that; he is their devoted guardian angel.'

She sipped her sherry, very aware of him sitting opposite her, Brontes pressed up against him, both of them watching her. Her tongue, as it sometimes did, ran away with her. 'Do you want to tell me something? Is that why you asked me to lunch?'

'Yes, to both your questions, but it can wait.' He settled back in his great chair. 'Your sister is a bright child; has she any ideas about the future?' It was a casual question and she answered readily enough.

'She's clever; she's set her heart on GCSEs, A levels, and a university.'

'Some discerning young man will snap her up long before then.' He smiled at her. 'And why aren't you married?'

It was unexpected. 'Well, I—I…that is, they weren't the right ones. None of them the right man.'

This muddled statement he received with a gentle smile. 'Have you any messages for Eloise?'

'If you would tell her that Peggy seems happy and is doing well at school and that everything is fine. She hasn't written or phoned, but I expect she's very busy.'

'Undoubtedly,' he agreed gravely. Peak came then to tell them that lunch was ready, and she went with the professor to a smaller room at the back of the house, which overlooked a surprisingly large garden. 'You've got trees, how lovely,' she exclaimed. 'It must look beautiful in the spring.'

They lunched off iced melon, baked salmon in a pastry case and a coffee *bavarois* and, while they ate, the professor kept the conversation quite firmly in his hands; impersonal topics, the kind of talk one might have had with a stranger sharing one's table in a restaurant, thought Francesca peevishly. Back in the drawing-room, drinking coffee from paper-thin cups, she said suddenly, 'I wish you would talk about your work—you looked different at the hospital; it's a side of you that I know nothing about.' She put down her cup. 'I'm sorry, I'm being nosy again.' She looked at her feet, aching in the shoes she longed to kick off. 'Only I'm interested,' she mumbled.

'I have an appointment at half-past two,' he told her. 'I'll drive you back as I go to my rooms, which means that we have half an hour. Do take off those shoes and curl up comfortably.'

'Oh, how did you know? I don't wear them very often and they're a bit tight. You don't mind?'

'Not in the least. What do you want to know about my work, Francesca?'

'Well, I know that you're a professor and a consultant, but are you a surgeon or a physician? You said you went to other hospitals and that you travelled. Why?'

'I'm a surgeon, open-heart surgery valve replacements, by-passes, transplants. Most of my work is at Regent's, but I operate at all the big provincial hospitals if I'm needed. I have a private practice and an out-patients clinic twice a week. I work in Leiden too, occasionally in Germany and the States, and from time to time in the Middle East.'

'Leiden,' said Francesca. 'You said *"tot ziens"* one morning in the park; we looked it up—it's Dutch.'

'My mother is a Dutchwoman; she lives just outside Leiden. I spend a good deal of time there. My father was British; he died two years ago.'

He looked at her, half smiling, one eyebrow raised in a gentle way. The half-smile widened and she thought it was mocking, and went red. He must think her a half-wit with no manners. She plunged into a muddled speech. 'I don't know why I had to be so rude, I do apologise, I have no excuse, if I were you I wouldn't want to speak to me again—'

He said gently, 'But I'm not you, and fortunately I see no reason why I shouldn't speak to you again. For one thing, it may be necessary from time to time. I did tell Eloise that I would keep an eye on Peggy.'

'Yes, of course. I—I expect that you would like to go now.' She sat up straight and crammed her feet back into her shoes and then stood up. 'Thank you for my lunch—it was delicious.'

He appeared not to notice how awkward she felt. Only as he stopped in Cornel Mews and got out to take the key from her and open the door of the cottage did he say, 'We must have another talk some time, Francesca,' and he bent to kiss her cheek as she went past him into the hall.

CHAPTER FOUR

FRANCESCA WAS sitting by the fire, reading to Peggy, when Lucy came in. 'Well, did you have a good lunch? What did you eat?'

Francesca recited the menu.

'Nice—to think I was chewing on liver and bacon... Where did you go?'

'To his house; it's quite close by.'

Lucy flung down her school books and knelt down by the fire. 'Tell me everything,' she demanded.

When Francesca had finished she said, 'He must be very rich. I expect he's clever too. I wonder what his mum's like.'

'How's school?'

'OK.' Lucy dug into a pocket. 'There's a letter for you, but don't take any notice of it; I don't want to go...'

The words were bravely said but palpably not true. A party of pupils was being organised to go skiing two weeks before Christmas. Two weeks in Switzerland with proper tuition and accompanied by teachers. The fare and the expenses totalled a sum which Francesca had no hope of finding.

'Oh, Lucy, I'm so sorry. If it's any consolation I'll get the money by hook or by crook for next winter.'

She glanced at her sister's resolutely cheerful face. 'All your friends are going?'

'Well, most of them, but I really don't mind, Fran. We can have a lovely time here, getting ready for Christmas.'

So nothing more was said about it, although Francesca sat up late, doing sums which, however hard she tried, never added up to enough money to pay for Lucy's skiing holiday. There was enough money set aside for her school fees, of course, but that wasn't to be touched. She went to bed finally with a headache.

There was no postcard from Mrs Vincent; nor was there a phone call. Francesca reminded herself that the professor would be with her, and most likely he would bring back something for Peggy when he returned. The child showed no concern at the absence of news from her mother, although it seemed to Francesca that she was looking pale and seemed listless; even Tom's antics were met with only a half-hearted response. Francesca consulted Mrs Wells. 'I think she should see a doctor. She isn't eating much either. I wonder if she's missing her mother...'

Mrs Wells gave her an old-fashioned look. 'I'm not one for telling tales out of school, but 'er mum never 'as had no time for 'er. Disappointed she was; she so pretty and charming and Peggy as plain as a pikestaff. No, you don't need to fret yerself about that, Miss Haley; little Peggy don't love 'er mum all that much. She was 'appier when her granny and grandpa came to visit. That was when Dr Vincent was alive—loved the child they did, and she loved them.'

So Francesca had done nothing for a few more days, although Peggy didn't seem any better. She had made up her mind to get a doctor by now. If only the professor had phoned, she could have asked his advice, but he, of course, would be wherever Mrs Vincent was. She fetched Peggy from school, gave her her tea which she didn't want and, as soon as Lucy came home, took the child upstairs to bed. Peggy felt hot and she wished she could take her temperature, but there was a singular lack of first-aid equipment in the house, and she blamed herself for not having attended to that. She sat the child on her lap and started to undress her, and as she took off her clothes she saw the rash. The small, thin back was covered with red spots. She finished the undressing, washed the pale little face, and brushed the mousy hair and tucked the child up in bed. 'A nice glass of cold milk,' she suggested, 'and Lucy shall bring it up to you.'

'Tom—I want Tom,' said Peggy in a small voice. 'I've got a pain in my head.'

'You shall have Tom, my dear,' said Francesca and sped downstairs, told Lucy, and went to the phone. Even if the professor were still away, surely that nice man Peak would have a phone number or, failing that, know of a local doctor.

She dialled the number Mrs Vincent had left in her desk and Peak answered.

'Peak, did Professor Pitt-Colwyn leave a phone number? I need to speak to him—Peggy's ill.'

'A moment, Miss Haley,' and a second later the professor's voice, very calm, sounded in her ear.

'Francesca?'

'Oh, so you are there,' she said fiercely. 'Peggy's ill; there's a rash all over her back and she feels sick and listless. She's feverish, but I can't find a thermometer anywhere and I don't know where there's a doctor and I've not heard a word since Mrs Vincent went away—'

'Peggy's in bed? Good. I'll be with you in about ten minutes.' He rang off and she spent a moment with the unhappy thought that she had been anything but calm and sensible; she had even been rather rude...and he had sounded impassive and impersonal, as though she were a patient to be dealt with efficiently. Though I'm not the patient, she thought in a muddled way as she went back to Peggy and sent Lucy downstairs to open the door for the professor, and then sat down on the side of the bed to hold the tearful child in her arms.

She didn't hear him come in; for such a big man he was both quick and silent. She was only aware of him when he put two hands on her shoulders and eased her away from Peggy and took her place.

He was unhurried and perfectly calm and apparently unworried and it was several minutes before he examined the child, took her temperature and then sat back while Francesca made her comfortable again. 'Have you had chicken-pox?' He glanced at Francesca.

'Me? Oh, yes, years ago; so has Lucy.'

'And so have I, and now so has Peggy.' He took the small, limp hand in his. 'You'll feel better very soon, Peggy. Everyone has chicken-pox, you know,

but it only lasts a few days. You will take the medicine Francesca will give you and then you'll sleep as
soundly as Tom and in the morning I'll come and see
you again.'

'I don't want Mummy to come home—'

'Well, love, there really is no need. Francesca will
look after you, and as soon as you feel better we'll
decide what is to happen next, shall we?' He kissed
the hot little head. 'Lucy will come and sit with you
until Francesca brings your medicine. *Tot ziens.*'

Peggy managed a watery smile and said, '*Tot
ziens.*'

In the sitting-room Francesca asked anxiously,
'She's not ill, is she? I mean, ill enough to let her
mother know? She said she didn't want to be—that
is, there was no need to ring her unless there was
something serious.'

When he didn't answer she added, 'I'm sorry if I
was rude on the phone; I was worried and I thought
you were away.'

'Now why should you think that?'

'You said you were going to Cheltenham.'

'As indeed I did go.' He was writing a prescription
as he spoke. 'Don't worry, Peggy is quite all right.
She has a temperature but, having chicken-pox, that
is only to be expected. Get this tomorrow morning
and see that she takes it three times a day.' He took
a bottle from his bag and shook out a tablet. 'This
will dissolve in hot milk; it will make her more comfortable and she should sleep.'

He closed his bag and stood up. 'I'll call in on my
way to the hospital in the morning, but if you're wor-

ried don't hesitate to phone me; I'll come at once.'
At the door he turned. 'And don't worry about her
mother. I'll be seeing her again in a day or so and
then I can reassure her.'

Francesca saw him to the door and wished him a
polite goodnight. If it hadn't been imperative that she
should see to Peggy at once, she would have gone
somewhere quiet and had a good cry. She wasn't sure
why she wanted to do this and there really wasn't
time to think about it.

Peggy slept all night and Francesca was up and
dressed and giving the little girl a drink of lemonade
when the professor arrived. He was in flannels and a
thick sweater and he hadn't shaved, and she said at
once, 'You've been up all night.'

'Not quite all of it. How is Peggy?'

They went to look at her together and he pronounced himself content with her progress. There
were more spots now, of course, but her temperature
was down a little and she greeted him cheerfully
enough. 'Anything in moderation if she's hungry,' he
told Francesca, 'and get the elixir started as soon as
you can.'

'Thank you for coming. Lucy's made tea—we
haven't had our breakfast yet. You'll have a cup?'

He refused pleasantly. 'I must get home and shower
and change; I've an out-patients clinic at ten o'clock.'

She opened the door onto a chilly morning.

'I'll look in some time this evening.' He was gone
with a casual nod.

It was late in the afternoon when Francesca had a
phone call from Peggy's grandmother in Wiltshire. It

was a nice, motherly voice with no hint of fussing. 'Renier telephoned. Poor little Peggy, but we are so glad to know that she is being so well looked after. I suppose you haven't heard from her mother?'

'Well, no, the professor said that he would be seeing her and that there was no need to let her know. Peggy is feeling much better and he is looking after her so well, so please don't be anxious.'

'She's our only grandchild and so like our son. He was Renier's friend, you know. They were at university together and school together—he was best man at their wedding and is godfather to Peggy.'

'Would you like to speak to Peggy? She's awake. I'll carry her across to the other bedroom; there's a phone there…'

'That would be delightful. Shall I ring off or wait?'

'If you would wait—I'll be very quick…'

The conversation went on for some time, with Peggy on Francesca's lap, talking non-stop and getting too excited. Presently Francesca whispered, 'Look, Peggy, ask Granny if you can telephone her each day about teatime, and if she says "yes" say goodbye now.'

A satisfactory arrangement for all parties.

The professor came in the evening, once more the epitome of the well-dressed gentleman. He was coolly polite to Francesca, spent ten minutes with Peggy, who was tired and a little peevish now, pronounced himself satisfied and, after only the briefest of conversations, went away again.

'No need to come in the morning,' he observed, 'but I'll take a look about this time tomorrow.'

The next day he told Francesca that Peggy might get up in her dressing-gown and roam the house. 'Keep her warm, she needs a week or so before she goes back to school. You're dealing with the spots, aren't you? She mustn't scratch.'

The next day he told her that he would be seeing Eloise on the following day.

'How nice,' said Francesca tartly. 'I'm sure you will be able to reassure her. Peggy's granny has been phoning each afternoon; she sounds just like a granny…' A silly remark, she realised, but she went on, 'Peggy's very fond of her.'

'Yes, I know. I shall do my best to persuade Eloise to let her go and stay with her for a few days. You will have to go too, of course.'

'But what about Lucy?'

'I imagine that it could be arranged for her to board for a week or so? Eloise will pay, of course. Would Lucy mind?'

'I think she would love it…but it will be quite an expense.'

'Not for Eloise, and Peggy will need someone with her.'

'What about Tom?'

'I'm sure that her grandmother will make him welcome. I'll let you know.'

He made his usual abrupt departure.

'Most unsatisfactory,' said Francesca to the empty room. She told Lucy, of course, who found it a marvellous idea. 'They have such fun, the boarders—and almost all of my friends are boarders. Do you suppose Mrs Vincent will pay for me?'

'Professor Pitt-Colwyn seemed to think she would. He's going to let me know…'

'Well, of course,' said Lucy airily. 'If they're in love they'll do anything to please each other. I bet you anything that he'll be back in a few days with everything arranged.'

She was right. Several days later he arrived at tea-time, just as they were sitting on the floor in front of the fire, toasting crumpets.

Peggy, no longer spotty but decidedly pasty-faced, rushed to meet him.

'Where have you been? I missed you. Francesca and Lucy missed you too.'

He picked her up and kissed her. 'Well, now I'm here, may I have a cup of tea and one of those crumpets? There's a parcel in the hall for you, too.' He put her down. 'Run and get it; it's from your mother.'

'Will you have a cup of tea?' asked Francesca in a hostess voice and, at his mocking smile and nod, went on, 'Peggy seems to be quite well again, no temperature for three days, but she's so pale…'

She came into the room then with the parcel and began to unwrap it without much enthusiasm. A doll—a magnificent creature, elaborately dressed.

'How very beautiful,' said Francesca. 'You must give her a name. What a lovely present from Mummy.'

'She's like all my other dolls and I don't like any of them. I like my teddy and Tom.' Peggy put the doll carefully on a chair and climbed on to the professor's lap. 'I had a crumpet,' she told him, 'but I can have some of yours, can't I?'

'Provided you don't drip butter all over me and Francesca allows it.'

Francesca passed a large paper serviette over without a word, and poured the fresh tea Lucy had made. That young lady settled herself on the rug before the fire once again and sank her teeth into a crumpet.

'Do tell,' she said. 'Is—?' She caught the professor's eye. 'Oh, yes, of course,' and went on airily, 'Did you have a nice time wherever you went?'

The professor, who had spent exactly twenty-four hours in Birmingham—a city he disliked—only four of which had been in Eloise's company, replied blandly that indeed he had had a most interesting time, as he had a flying visit to Edinburgh and, since heart transplants had often to be dealt with at the most awkward of hours, an all-night session there and, upon his return, another operation in the early hours of the morning at Regent's. Francesca, unaware of this, of course, allowed her imagination to run riot.

She said waspishly, 'I expect a man in your position can take a holiday more or less when he likes. Have another crumpet?'

He took one and allowed Peggy to bite from it before demolishing it.

'There are no more crumpets, I'm afraid,' said Francesca coldly, 'but there is plenty of bread. I can make toast...'

He was sitting back with his eyes closed. 'Delicious—well buttered and spread with Marmite. You know the way to a man's heart, Francesca.'

He opened one eye and smiled at her, but she pretended not to see that and went away to fetch some bread and a pot of Marmite. She put the kettle on again too, foreseeing yet another pot of tea.

The other three were talking about Christmas and laughing a great deal when she got back, and it wasn't until he had at last eaten everything he had been offered that he exchanged a glance with Lucy, who got up at once. 'Peggy! Help me take everything into the kitchen, will you, and we'll wash up? You can have an apron and do the washing; I'll dry.'

Peggy scrambled off the professor's knee. 'You'll not go away?'

'No. What is more, if I'm allowed to, I'll stay until you're in your bed.'

Left alone with him, Francesca cast around in her head for a suitable topic of conversation and came up with, 'Did Mrs Vincent give you any messages for me?'

'None. She thinks it a splendid idea that Peggy should go to her grandmother's for a week or so and that you will go with her. She is quite willing to pay for Lucy to stay at school during that time since she is inconveniencing you. She has asked me to make the arrangements and deal with the travelling and payment of bills and so forth. Oh, and she wishes Mrs Wells to come each day as usual while you're away.'

'Tom Kitten...?'

'He can surely go with you; I can't imagine that Peggy will go without him.'

'No. I'm sure she wouldn't. You reassured Mrs Vincent about Peggy not being well? She's not worried?'

The professor had a brief memory of Eloise's pretty

face turning petulant at the threat of her new, exciting life being disrupted. 'No,' he said quietly. 'She is content to leave Peggy in your charge.'

'When are we to go?'

'Sunday morning. That gives you three days in which to pack and leave everything as you would wish it here. I'll telephone Mrs Vincent and talk to her about it; I know that she will be delighted.'

'It won't be too much work for her?'

'She and Mr Vincent have plenty of help. Besides, they love Peggy.'

'Am I to ask Lucy's headmistress if she can board for a week or two?'

'I'll attend to that as well.'

Lucy and Peggy came back then. 'I've washed up,' piped Peggy importantly, 'and now I'm going to have a bath and go to bed. I'll be so very very quick and if you like you can see where my spots were.'

'I look forward to that,' he assured her gravely. 'In ten minutes' time.'

He went as soon as Peggy, bathed and in her nightgown, had solemnly shown him the faint scars from her spots and then bidden him a sleepy goodnight.

His goodbyes were brief, with the remark that he would telephone some time on Saturday to make final arrangements for Sunday.

Lucy was over the moon; she was popular at school and had many friends and, although she had never said so, Francesca was aware that she would like to have been a boarder, and, as for Peggy, when she was told there was no containing her excitement. Something of their pleasure rubbed off on to Francesca and she found herself looking forward to the visit. The future seemed uncertain: there was still no word from Mrs Vincent, although Peggy had had a postcard from Carlisle. There had been no message on it, merely a scrawled, 'Hope you are being a good girl, love Mummy.'

Francesca's efforts to get Peggy to make a crayon drawing for her mother or buy a postcard to send to her came to nought. She wrote to Mrs Vincent's solicitor, enclosing a letter to her and asking him to forward it. She gave a faithful account of Peggy's progress and enclosed an accurate rendering of the money she had spent from the housekeeping allowance, assured her that the little girl was quite well again and asked her to let her know if there was anything special she wished done. The solicitor replied immediately; he understood from Mrs Vincent that it was most unlikely that she would be returning home for some time and Miss Haley was to do whatever she thought was best for Peggy. It wasn't very satisfactory, but Francesca realised that she would have to make the best of it. At least she could call upon the professor again if anything went wrong, and, now that they were going to stay with Peggy's grandparents for a while, they would surely accept responsibility for the child.

The professor telephoned quite early on Saturday morning; he would take Lucy to her school and at the same time have a word with the headmistress. 'Just to make sure that everything is in order,' he explained in what Francesca described to herself as his soothing voice.

'Should I go with you?' she wanted to know.

'No need. I dare say you've already had a few words with her.'

Francesca, feeling guilty, said that yes, she had. 'Just about her clothes and so on,' she said placatingly, and was answered by a mocking grunt.

He arrived on the doorstep in the afternoon with Brontes sitting on the back seat, greeted her with casual civility, assured Peggy that he would take her to her granny's in the morning, waited while Lucy bade Francesca goodbye at some length and then drove her away, refusing politely to return for tea. 'I'm expecting a call from Eloise,' he explained, watching Francesca's face.

Lucy telephoned in the evening; she sounded happy and any doubts that Francesca might have had about her sister's feeling homesick were swept away. She promised to phone herself when they arrived at Peggy's grandparents' house and went away to finish packing.

The professor arrived in time for coffee which Mrs Wells, who had popped round to take the keys and lock up, had ready. He was in an affable mood, answering Peggy's questions with patience while Brontes brooded in a kindly fashion over Tom. Francesca drank her coffee and had nothing to say, conscious that just having the professor there was all she wanted; he annoyed her excessively at times and she didn't think that he liked her overmuch but, all the same, when he was around she felt that there was no need for her to worry about anything. The future was vague—once Mrs Vincent came home she would be out of work again—but then in the meantime she was saving almost every penny of her wages and she liked her job. Moreover, she had become very fond of Peggy.

Rather to her surprise, she was told to sit in the front of the car. 'Brontes will take care of Peggy,' said the professor. 'Tom can sit in the middle in his basket.'

She stayed prudently silent until they joined the M4 where he put a large, well-shod foot down and allowed the car to slide past everything else in the fast lane. 'Just where are we going?' she asked a shade tartly.

'Oh, dear, did I not tell you? But you do know Wiltshire?' When she nodded he added, 'Just on the other side of the Berkshire border. Marlborough is the nearest town. The village is called Nether Tawscombe. They live in the Old Rectory, a charming old place.'

'You've been there before?'

He laughed shortly. 'I spent a number of school holidays there with Jeff and later, when we were at Cambridge and medical school, we spent a good deal of time there.'

'Then he got married,' prompted Francesca.

'Yes. Eloise was never happy there; she dislikes the country.'

Something in his voice stopped her from saying anything more; she turned round to see how the occupants of the back seat were getting on. Peggy had an arm round Brontes's great neck, she had stuck the fingers of her other hand through the mesh in front of Tom's basket and wore an expression of happiness which turned her plain little face into near prettiness. Francesca, who had had secret doubts about the visit, knew that she had been mistaken.

They arrived at Nether Tawscombe in time for lunch. The one village street was empty under the thin, wintry sunshine, but the houses which lined it looked charming. They got larger as the street went uphill until it reached the church, surrounded by a churchyard and ringed around by fair-sized houses. The Old Rectory was close by; an open gate led to a low, rambling house with diamond-paned windows and a solid front door.

As the professor stopped before it, it was opened and an elderly man came to meet them. She stood a little on one side until Peggy's excited greetings were over and the two men had shaken hands. She was led indoors while the professor saw to their baggage. The hall was stone-flagged, long and narrow, with a door opening on to the garden at the back of the house at its end. Brontes had made straight for it and had been joined by a black Labrador, who had rushed out of an open doorway as a grey-haired lady, cosily plump, had come into the hall.

Peggy screamed with delight and flung herself at her grandmother, and Mr Vincent said to Francesca, 'Always had a soft spot for each other—haven't had her to stay for a long time. This is delightful, Miss—er…?'

'Would you call me Francesca, please? Peggy does.'

Mrs Vincent came to take her hand then, with a

warmth which caused sudden tears to prick her eye-lids, for the last few years she had been without that kindly warmth...

That the professor was an old friend and welcome guest was evident: he hugged Mrs Vincent, asked which rooms the bags were to go to, and went up the wide staircase with the air of a man who knew his way about blindfold.

Mrs Vincent saw Francesca's eyes follow him and said comfortably, 'We've known Renier for many years. He and our son were friends; he spent many a school holiday here and Jeff went over to Holland. He's a good man, but I suspect you've discovered that for yourself, Miss...may I call you Francesca?'

'Oh, yes, please. What would you like me to do? Take Peggy upstairs and tidy her for lunch? She's so happy and excited.'

'Yes, dear. You do exactly what you've been do-ing. We know so little about her day-to-day life now that her father is dead—he brought her here very of-ten, you see.'

No mention of Eloise, reflected Francesca. It wasn't her business, of course. She bore Peggy away upstairs to a couple of low-ceilinged rooms with a commu-nicating door and windows overlooking the wintry garden beyond. After London, even the elegant part of London, it was sheer bliss.

The professor stayed to lunch and she was mysti-fied to hear him say that no, he wasn't going back to London.

'Having a quiet weekend at Pomfritt Cleeve?

Splendid,' observed Mr Vincent, and most annoyingly said no more about it.

Renier took his leave soon after lunch, saying goodbye to Francesca last of all, patting her shoulder in an avuncular fashion and remarking casually that he would probably see her at some time. She stood in the hall with everyone else, wishing with all her heart that she were going with him. For that was where she wanted to be, she realised with breathtaking surprise, with him all the time, forever and ever, and, now she came to think about it, she had been in love with him for quite some time, only she had never allowed herself to think about it. Now he was going; not that that would make any difference—he had always treated her at best with friendliness, more often than not with an uninterested politeness. She looked away so that she didn't see him go through the door.

However sad the state of her heart, she had little time to brood over it. Peggy was a different child, behaving like any normal six-year-old would behave, playing endless games with the Labrador and Tom, racing around the large garden with Francesca in laughing pursuit, going for rides on the elderly donkey who lived in the paddock behind the house, going to the shops in Marlborough with her grandmother and Francesca. She had quickly acquired a splendid appetite and slept the moment her small head touched the pillow. A good thing too, thought Francesca, for by bedtime she was tired herself. She loved her days in the quiet village and Mr and Mrs Vincent treated her like a daughter. Sometimes she felt guilty that she should be living so comfortably while Lucy was in

London, although she thought that her sister, from all accounts, was as happy as she was herself. They missed each other, but Francesca had the sense to see that it was good for Lucy to learn independence. She tried not to think of the professor too often and she felt that she was succeeding, until after a week or so Lucy wrote her usual letter and mentioned that he had been to see her at the school and had taken her out to tea. 'To the Ritz, no less!' scrawled Lucy, with a lot of exclamation marks.

The professor, having returned Lucy to her school, went to his home and sat down in his great chair by the fire with Brontes pressed against his knee and mother cat and the kittens asleep in their basket to keep him company. Tea with Lucy had been rewarding and he had made no bones about asking questions, although he had put them in such a way that she hadn't been aware of how much she was telling him. Indeed, she had confided in him that her headmistress had offered her a place in a group of girls from her class going to Switzerland for a skiing holiday. 'But of course I can't go,' she had told him. 'It's a lot of money and Fran couldn't possibly afford it—I mean, we both have to have new winter coats, and if Mrs Vincent comes back we'll have to move again, won't we?'

He had agreed with her gravely, at the same time prising out as much information about the trip as he could. He stroked Brontes's great head. 'I shall have to pay another visit to Eloise,' he told the dog. 'Now how can I fit that in next week?'

Presently he picked up the telephone on the table beside him and dialled a number.

A week, ten days went by. Peggy was so happy that Francesca began to worry about their return; she saw that the child loved her grandparents and they in turn loved her. They didn't spoil her, but she was treated with a real affection which Francesca felt she had never had from her mother. One morning when Peggy had gone off with her grandfather, leaving Francesca to catch up on the washing and ironing of the child's wardrobe, Mrs Vincent came to sit with her in the little room behind the kitchen where the ironing was done. 'You must be wondering why we don't mention Peggy's mother. Oh, I know we talk about her because Peggy must not forget her mother, but you see Eloise never wanted her and when she was born she turned against her—you see she takes after my son, and Eloise was so pretty. She said that her friends would laugh at such an ugly child. It upset Jeff, but she was fortunate—he was a loyal husband; he took Peggy around with him as much as possible and they adored each other. It was a pity that Peggy overheard her mother telling someone one day that she wished the child had not been born. She never told her father, bless the child, but she did tell Mrs Wells, who told me. There is nothing I would like better than to have Peggy to live with us always.'

'Have you suggested it to Eloise?'

'No; you see she will probably marry again and he might like to have Peggy for a daughter.'

Francesca thought Mrs Vincent was talking about

the professor. She said woodenly, 'Yes, I dare say that would be very likely.'

It seemed as though it might be true, for the very next day he arrived just as they were sitting down to lunch.

Francesca, going out to the kitchen to ask Bertha, the housekeeper, if she could grill another few chops for their unexpected guest, was glad of her errand: it gave her time to assume the politely cool manner she could hide behind. It was difficult to maintain it, though, for when she got back to the dining-room it was to hear him telling the Vincents that he was on his way to see Eloise. 'I shall be glad of a word with you, sir,' he told Mr Vincent, 'as my visit concerns Peggy, and I think you should know why I am going.'

Francesca ate her chop—sawdust and ashes in her mouth. Afterwards she couldn't remember eating it; nor could she remember what part she took in the conversation during the meal. It must have been normal, for no one looked at her in surprise. She couldn't wait for the professor to be gone, and as though he knew that he sat over coffee, teasing Peggy and having a perfectly unnecessary conversation with Mrs Vincent about the uses of the old-fashioned remedies she used for minor ailments.

He got up at length and went away with Mr Vincent to the study, to emerge half an hour later and, amid a great chorus of goodbyes, take his leave.

This time Francesca watched him go; when next she saw him he would most likely be engaged to Eloise—even married. She was vague about special licences but, the professor being the man he was, she had no doubt that if he wished to procure one at a moment's notice he would find a way to do so.

It was three days later when Mr Vincent remarked to his wife, 'Renier phoned. He has got his way. He's back in London, but too busy to come down and see us for a few days.'

Mrs Vincent beamed. 'Tell me later—how delightful; he must be very happy.' Francesca, making a Plasticine cat for Peggy, did her best to feel happy, because he was happy, and one should be glad to know that someone one loved was happy, shouldn't one? She found it hard work.

He came at the end of the week, walking in unannounced during a wet afternoon. He looked tired; he worked too hard, thought Francesca lovingly, scanning the weary lines on his handsome face. He also looked smug—something she found hard to understand.

CHAPTER FIVE

RENIER HAD HAD LUNCH, he assured Mrs Vincent, before going with Mr Vincent to the study again. When they came back into the sitting-room the older man said, 'Well, my dear, it's all settled. Which of us shall tell Peggy?'

'What?' asked Peggy, all ears. 'Is—is it something nice? Like I can stay here forever?'

'You clever girl to guess,' said Mrs Vincent, and gave her a hug. 'That's exactly what you are going to do—live here with Grandpa and me and go to school every day.'

Peggy flung herself at her grandfather. 'Really, truly? I may stay here with you? I won't have to go back to Mummy? She doesn't want me, you know.'

'Well, darling, your mummy is a very busy person and being on stage is very hard work. You can go and see her whenever you want to,' said Mrs Vincent.

'Shan't want to. Where will Francesca go?'

Francesca went on fixing a tail to another cat and didn't look up. 'If there is no objection, I think it might be a good idea if I took her somewhere quiet and explained everything to her,' said the professor.

He added gently, 'Get your coat, Francesca, and come with me.'

'Now that is a good idea,' said Mrs Vincent. 'Run

along, dear; Renier will explain everything to you so much better than we can.'

There was no point in refusing; she fetched her old Burberry and went out to the car with him, to be greeted with pleasure by Brontes, who was roaming the garden. The professor opened the door and stuffed her gently into her seat, got in beside her and, with Brontes's great head wedged between their shoulders, drove off.

'Where am I going?' asked Francesca coldly.

'Pomfritt Cleeve. I have a cottage there. We can talk quietly.'

'What about? Surely you could have told me at Mrs Vincent's house?'

'No, this concerns you as well as Peggy.'

He had turned off the main road into a narrow, high-hedged lane going downhill, and presently she saw a cluster of lights through the gathering dusk. A minute or so later they had reached the village—one street with a church halfway along, a shop or two, and small, old cottages, well maintained—before he turned into another narrow lane, and after a hundred yards or so drove through a propped-open gate and stopped before a thatched cottage of some size. There were lights in the windows and the door was thrown open as she got out of the car, hesitating for a moment, giving Brontes time to rush through the door with a delighted bark, almost knocking down the stout little lady standing there. She said, 'Good doggie,' in a soft, West Country voice and then added, 'Come on in out of the cold, sir, and the young lady. There's a good fire in the sitting-room and tea in ten minutes.'

The professor flung an arm around her cosy person

and kissed her soundly. 'Blossom, how very nice to see you again—and something smells delicious.'

He caught Francesca gently by the arm. 'Francesca, this is Blossom, who lives here and looks after the cottage for me. Blossom, this is Miss Haley. Take her away so that she can tidy herself if she wants to, and we'll have tea in ten minutes, just as you say.'

The cottage, decided Francesca, wasn't a cottage really. It might look like one, but it was far too big to warrant such a name, although there was nothing grand about it. The sitting-room to which she was presently shown was low-ceilinged with comfortable chairs and tables dotted around on the polished floor. There was a low table before the fire and sofas on either side of it. She sat opposite her host, pouring tea into delicate china cups and eating scones warm from the oven and, having been well brought up, made light conversation.

However, not for long. 'Let us dispense with the small talk,' said the professor, 'and get down to facts. Eloise is quite happy to allow Peggy to live with her grandparents. She will of course be free to see the child whenever she wishes, but she will remarry very shortly and intends to stay on the stage, so it isn't likely that she will visit Peggy more than once in a while. Mrs Vincent will employ her old nanny's daughter to look after Peggy, so you may expect to leave as soon as she arrives.' Francesca gave a gasp, but he went on, 'Don't interrupt, I have not yet finished. Lucy has been told that she may join a school party going to Switzerland to ski—I have seen her headmistress and she will join the party.'

'Now look here,' said Francesca, and was hushed once more.

'I haven't said anything to you, for I knew that you would refuse to do anything about it. The child deserves a holiday and, as for the costs, you can repay me when you are able.'

'But I haven't got a job,' said Francesca wildly. 'I never heard such arrogance—going behind my back and making plans and arranging things—'

'Ah, yes, as to arrangements for yourself, Eloise is quite agreeable to your remaining at the cottage for a few days so that you can pack your things.'

She goggled at him, bereft of words. That she loved him dearly went without saying, but at the moment she wished for something solid to throw at him. 'You have been busy, haven't you?' she said nastily.

'Yes, indeed I have. I shall drive Lucy over to Zeebrugge to meet the school party there; you would like to come with us, no doubt.'

'How can I? I'll have to look for a job—'

'Well, as to that, I have a proposal to make.' He was sitting back, watching her, smiling faintly.

'Well, I don't want to hear it,' she declared roundly. 'I shan't listen to anything more you may say—'

'Perhaps this isn't the right time, after all. You are cross, are you not? But there is really nothing you can do about it, is there? You will break young Lucy's heart if you refuse to let her go to Switzerland—'

'She had no skiing clothes.'

'Now she has all she needs—a Christmas present.'

She all but ground her teeth. 'And I suppose you're going to get married?'

'That is my intention.'

Rage and despair almost choked her, and she allowed rage to take over.

'I hope you will be very happy.' Her voice was icy and not quite steady.

'I am certain of that.'

'I'd like to go back.' He agreed at once, which was a good thing—otherwise she might have burst into tears. Where was she to go? And there was Lucy to think of when she got back from Switzerland. Would she have time to get a job by then? And would her small hoard of money be sufficient to keep them until she had found work again? There were so many questions to be answered. Perhaps she should have listened to this proposal he had mentioned—it could have been another job—but pride wouldn't allow her to utter another word. She bade Blossom goodbye, complimented her on her scones and got into the car; it smelled comfortingly of leather and, very faintly, of Brontes.

Strangely enough, the great bulk of the professor beside her was comforting too, although she could think of no good reason why it should be.

Back at the Vincent's house after a silent drive, he bade them goodbye, bent his great height to Peggy's hug, observed cheerfully to Francesca that he would be in touch, and left.

She had no idea what he had said to the Vincents, but from what they said she gathered that they understood her to have a settled future, and there seemed no point in enlightening them. Peggy, chattering excitedly as Francesca put her to bed, seemed to think that she would see her as often as she wanted, and Francesca said nothing to disillusion her. The future was her own problem.

She left the Vincents two days later, and was driven back to the mews cottage by Mr Vincent. She hated leaving the quiet village. Moreover, she had grown very fond of Peggy who, even while bidding her a tearful goodbye, was full of plans to see her again, which were seconded by her grandmother. She had responded suitably and kept up a cheerful conversation with her companion as they drove but, once he had left her at the empty house, with the observation that they would be seeing each other shortly, she sat down in the kitchen and had a good cry. She felt better after that, made a cup of tea, and unpacked before starting on the task of re-packing Lucy's cases as well as her own. There had been a brief letter for her before she left the Vincents', telling her that they would be crossing over to Zeebrugge in two days' time, and would she be ready to leave by nine o'clock in the morning and not a minute later?

Mrs Wells had kept the place spotless, and there was a note on the kitchen table saying that she would come in the morning; there was a little ironing and nothing else to do but pack. She was halfway through that when Lucy phoned.

'You're back. Isn't it exciting? I can't believe it's true. I'm coming home tomorrow afternoon. The bus leaves here in the evening, but Renier says he'll take us to Zeebrugge early the next day and I can join the others there. Isn't he a darling?' She didn't wait for Francesca's answer, which was just as well. 'Oh, Fran, I do love being a boarder. I know I can't be, but you have no idea what fun it is. I've been asked to lots of parties at Christmas, too.'

Francesca let her talk. There was time enough to worry over the problem of Christmas; she still had almost three weeks to find a job and somewhere for them to live, too.

'You're very quiet,' said Lucy suddenly.

'I've had a busy day; I'm packing for us both now—I'll do the rest tomorrow. I've got to talk to Mrs Wells, too.'

'I'll help you. You are looking forward to the trip, aren't you?'

'Tremendously,' said Francesca with her fingers crossed. 'See you tomorrow, Lucy.'

By the time Lucy arrived, she had done everything that was necessary. Mrs Wells had been more than helpful, arranging to come early in the morning to take the keys and lock up. The solicitor had been dealt with, she had been to the bank and taken out as much money as she dared, found their passports—unused since they had been on holiday in France with their parents—and, finally, written a letter to Mrs Vincent which she had enclosed in a letter to the solicitor. There was nothing more to do but have a good gossip and go to bed.

The Bentley purred to a halt outside the cottage at precisely nine o'clock, then the professor got out, wished them an affable good-morning, put Francesca's overnight bag and Lucy's case in the boot, enquired as to what had been done with the rest of their luggage—safely with Mrs Wells—and urged them to get in. 'You go in front, Lucy,' said Francesca and nipped into the back seat, not seeing his smile, and resolutely looked out of the window all the way to Dover, trying not to listen to the cheerful talk between the other two.

Five hours later they were in Zeebrugge, driving to the hotel where the rest of the party had spent the night, and it was only then that she realised that she had no idea what was to happen next. There wasn't any time to think about it; the bus was ready to leave. It was only after a hasty goodbye to Lucy, when she was watching the party drive away, that the full awkwardness of the situation dawned upon her. 'Whatever am I going to do?' She had turned on the professor, her voice shrill with sudden fright. 'When is there a boat back?'

He took her arm. 'We are going to my home in Holland for the night. My mother will be delighted to meet you.'

'I must get back—I have to find a job.'

He took no notice, merely urged her gently into the car, got in beside her and drove off.

'This is ridiculous…I've been a fool—I thought we would be going straight back. I'm to spend the night at Mrs Wells's house.'

'We will telephone her.' His voice was soothing as well as matter-of-fact. 'We shall soon be home.'

They were already through Brugge and on the motorway, bypassing Antwerp, crossing into Holland, and racing up the Dutch motorways to Tilburg, Nijmegen and on past Arnhem. The wintry afternoon was turning to an early dusk and, save for a brief halt for coffee and sandwiches, they hadn't stopped. Francesca, trying to make sense of the situation, sat silent, her mind addled with tiredness and worry and a deep-seated misery, because once they were back in England there would be no reason to see the professor ever again. The thought cast her in such deep gloom that she barely noticed the country had changed; the road ran through trees and thick shrubbery with a light glimpsed here and there. The professor turned off the road through a gateway, slowed along a narrow, sanded drive and stopped before the house at its end. He leaned over, undid her safety belt, got out and helped her out too, and she stood for a moment, looking at the dark bulk of the house. It was square and solid, its big windows lighted, frost sparkling on the iron balcony above the porch.

She said in a forlorn voice, 'I should never have come with you. I should never have let you take over my life, and Lucy's, too. I'm very grateful for your help; you have been kind and I expect it suited you and Eloise. I can't think why you've brought me here.'

'You wouldn't listen to my proposal at Pomfritt Cleeve,' the professor had come very close, 'I can see that I shall have to try again.' He put his arms around her and held her very close. 'You are a stubborn, proud girl with a beautiful head full of muddled thoughts, and I love you to distraction. I fell in love with you the first time I saw you, and what is all this nonsense about Eloise? I don't even like the woman, but something had to be done about Peggy. Now you will listen, my darling, while I make you a proposal. Will you marry me?'

What with his great arms around her and her heart thumping against her ribs, Francesca hadn't much breath—only just enough to say, 'Yes, oh, yes, Renier,' before he bent to kiss her.

MAKING SURE
OF SARAH

BY
BETTY NEELS

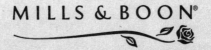
MILLS & BOON®

CHAPTER ONE

SARAH looked out of the car's windows at the flat, peaceful countryside of Holland, no longer listening to her stepfather's angry voice blaming everyone and everything but himself for getting lost. Her mother, sitting beside him with the map, had been ignored when she had pointed out the road they should have taken, but the main butt of his ill humour was Sarah.

He turned his red, angry face and said over his shoulder, 'You must have known that we had taken a wrong turning—why didn't you say so?'

Sarah said in her quiet voice, 'I don't know Holland. I came with you and Mother because you wanted someone who could speak French while you were in France.' She added before he could reply, 'If you had told us that you intended going back home through Belgium and Holland I would have bought a Dutch dictionary—so that I could have asked the way,' she pointed out in a matter-of-fact voice.

'Don't annoy your father, dear,' said her mother.

'He isn't my father; he's my stepfather,' said Sarah, and she wondered why her mother, after ten years or more, could bear to be married to him, and why she expected Sarah to think of him as her father. It had been mutual dislike at first sight, but her mother, who had managed to go through life turning a blind eye to anything which upset her, had steadfastly pretended that her ill-tempered husband and the daughter she had never quite understood were the best of friends.

Then, because she loved her mother, Sarah added, 'There was a road sign a mile or so back. It said "Arnhem, seventeen kilometres".'

'Why didn't you say so?' asked her stepfather furiously. 'Letting me drive miles out of my way.'

'I did. You told me not to bother you.'

He drove on then, muttering under his breath. Sarah turned a deaf ear, vaguely aware of her mother's conciliatory murmurs, uneasy now since he was driving much too fast. The road was narrow, with a ditch on either side and fields beyond; it stretched ahead of them with nothing in sight and the March day was drawing to a close. She thanked heaven silently that there were no curves or corners, and no traffic at all.

She had overlooked the ditches. Her stepfather, never a good driver, and an even worse one when he was in a bad temper, took a hand off the wheel to snatch the map from his wife's lap, and the car shot over the narrow grass verge and tumbled into the ditch.

The ditch was half filled with water draining from the fields, and the car hit the muddy bottom with tremendous force, its bonnet completely buried.

Sarah, flung hither and thither and ending up rather the worse for wear, still in her seat belt, was too shocked to speak, but it was, in a way, reassuring to hear her stepfather swearing, and then shouting, 'Get me out, get me out!'

Typical! thought Sarah, light-headed. What about Mother…? She came to then, scrambling round until she could undo the belt and lean over the seat where her mother was. Her mother was slumped over, her head against the dashboard, and she didn't answer when Sarah spoke to her. Sarah leaned over and found her arm and felt for her pulse—beating, she was relieved to find, reasonably strong. Her stepfather gave another shout, and she said loudly, 'Be quiet, do. Get out and help Mother, she's hurt…'

'You stupid girl. *I'm* hurt—my leg, my chest. Never mind your mother for the moment, go and get help. Be quick. Heaven knows how badly injured I am.'

'This is your fault,' said Sarah, 'and all you can think of is that you're hurt. Well, so is Mother…'

She wriggled out of her seat, and after a struggle managed to open the door of the car. The water, icy cold and thick with mud, came up to her knees, but she hardly noticed that. It was late afternoon and the sky was grey, but there was still plenty of light. She tugged at the handle of the door by her mother and found it jammed, so got back into the car again and leaned over to open it from inside. It didn't budge.

Frantically she managed to undo her mother's seat belt and haul her gently into a more comfortable position, relieved to feel her pulse was stronger now. There were rugs in the boot, but first she must turn off the engine, still running, and take a look at her stepfather. She hung over the back of his seat and managed to undo his seat belt and sit him up a little, not listening to his roars of rage.

And all this had taken only a few minutes, she realised, edging her way round to the boot and finding it thankfully burst open and the rugs easy to reach. She tucked them round her mother and stepfather and then scrambled up the bank and took a look. The flat countryside stretched round her, wide fields divided by ditches, a few trees, and not a house in sight. There was a clump of larger trees some way off. Perhaps there would be a farm there, but surely even on this quiet road there would be traffic or something, someone…

There was; still far off, but coming towards her, was a horse and cart. Sarah shouted then, and waved and shouted again until she was hoarse, but the cart didn't increase its speed. She didn't dare to leave her mother and stepfather, and watched it in an agony of impatience as the beast plodded steadily towards her. When the cart was near enough she ran towards it.

The man holding the reins halted the horse and stared down at her.

'An accident,' said Sarah. 'Police, ambulance, hospital.' And, since he didn't seem to understand her, she said it all again and added, 'Please, hurry…'

The man had a broad, dull face but he looked kind. He looked across at the upended car and then back at Sarah. *'Politie?'*

'Yes, yes. Please, hurry…'

He nodded then, thought for a moment, and broke into speech. It was a pity that she couldn't understand a word of it, but he ended with the word *politie* and urged his horse forward. Sarah watched the cart disappear slowly into the distance until the clump of trees hid it from view, and then she climbed back into the ditch.

Her mother was moaning a little, and Sarah tucked the rug more tightly around her and contrived to shift her legs so that they were free of the cold water which filled the front of the car. She tried to do the same for her stepfather, but one leg was at an awkward angle and she didn't dare to touch it. She made him as comfortable as possible and climbed out of the ditch once more, to meet a heartening sight: the blue flashing lights of a police car coming at speed.

The two men in it were large, reassuringly calm, and spoke English. She wanted to fling herself on a broad chest and burst into tears of relief, but it didn't seem the right moment.

'My mother and stepfather are in the car,' she told them, in a voice which shook only slightly. 'They're hurt. Is an ambulance coming?'

'It comes at once. And you, miss? You are not hurt?' the older of the two officers asked her.

'No, I'm fine.' She peered anxiously over the edge of the ditch to where the other officer was bending over her mother. She would have joined him, but the ambulance arrived then and she was urged to stand on one side while the policemen and the paramedics began the task of getting her mother and stepfather out of the car.

They were hefty men, and made short work of breaking down the car door, releasing her mother and lifting her into the ambulance. Getting her stepfather out was more difficult. His leg was broken and he was cut by broken glass, moreover he disputed their actions, shouting and swearing. Sarah was sorry that he was injured, but she hoped that the men would put his uninhibited behaviour down to shock.

It was almost dark now. While they had been busy, Sarah had unloaded their cases from the boot and stood with them, waiting to be told what to do next.

'You will come with us to the hospital,' said the older constable. 'We will take your luggage to the police station and tomorrow you may come and fetch it.' He waved the ambulance away and opened the car door for her. 'You have everything, passports, money?'

'Yes, I've put them in one of the cases. Where are we going?'

'Arnhem.' He gave her a brief glance. 'You are OK?'

Sarah said, 'Yes, thank you.' She was alive, unhurt, although she was aware of aches and pains and wet and icy feet and legs; she was OK.

The hospital at Arnhem was large and modern, and the Accident Room was heaving with people. The two policemen set her down beside the ambulance, warned her to collect the cases from the police station in the morning and be ready to give a report of the accident, and sped on their way. She watched them go with regret; they had been briskly friendly—warning her stepfather that they would come to the hospital to see him in the morning, patting her on the shoulder in a kindly fashion—and now they had gone, siren sounding, blue lights flashing. Another accident?

Sarah followed the two stretchers into the hospital and presently found herself in a waiting room with a lot of other anxious people. Someone would come and report on her mother and stepfather, she was told by a busy nurse, taking down particulars and thankfully speaking English.

Sarah settled into one of the plastic chairs arranged around the room. Her feet were numb now, and she smelled horrible. A cup of tea, she thought longingly, and a nice warm bath and then bed. She was hungry, too, and she felt guilty about that with her mother and stepfather injured. People came and went. Slowly the room emptied. Surely someone would come for her soon. She closed her eyes on a daydream of endless pots of tea and plates piled high with hot buttered toast and slept.

Mr ter Breukel, consultant orthopaedic surgeon at the hospital, finished his examination of Mr Holt's leg and bent his massive person over his patient. He studied the ill-tempered face and listened patiently to the diatribe directed at himself, his staff and everyone in general.

When Mr Holt drew breath, he said quietly, 'You have a broken leg; it will need to be pinned and plated. You have two broken ribs, a sprained wrist, and superficial cuts and bruises. You will be put to bed presently and in the morning I will set the leg. You will need to stay here until it is considered expedient to return you to England.'

Mr Holt said furiously, 'I demand to be sent to England immediately. How am I to know that you are competent to deal with my injuries? I am a businessman and have some influential friends.'

Mr ter Breukel ignored the rudeness. 'I will see you

in the morning. Your wife will be warded also. She has concussion but is not seriously hurt.'

He waited for Mr Holt to say something, and when he didn't added, 'Was there anyone else with you?'

'My stepdaughter.' Mr Holt gave him a look of deep dislike. 'She's quite capable of taking care of herself.'

'In the circumstances,' said Mr ter Breukel, 'that is most fortunate.'

The Accident Room was emptying, so he could safely leave the minor cases to the two casualty officers on duty, but first he supposed he should find this stepdaughter. Probably with her mother…

Mrs Holt was fully conscious now, and complaining weakly. She had no wish to stay in hospital; she must have a private room, she wanted her own nightclothes, her own toiletries…

Mr ter Breukel bent over the stretcher, lifted a limp hand and took her pulse. It was steady and quite strong. 'Your daughter?' he asked quietly. 'She was with you in the car?'

'Yes, yes, of course. Where is she? Why isn't she here with me? She knows how bad my nerves are. Someone must fetch her. She must find a good hotel where I can stay for a few days until my husband can return to England.'

'Mr Holt will have to remain here for some time, Mrs Holt, and I cannot allow you to leave this hospital until you have recovered from a slight concussion.'

'How tiresome.' Mrs Holt turned her head away and closed her eyes.

Mr ter Breukel nodded to the porters to wheel her away to the ward and went in search of the third member of the party.

The place was quieter now, and the waiting room was empty save for Sarah. He stood looking at her—such an ordinary girl, dirty and dishevelled, a bruise on one cheek and smelling vilely of the mud clinging to her person. A girl without looks, pale, her hair hanging in untidy damp streamers around a face which could easily pass unnoticed in a crowd. A girl completely lacking in glamour.

He sighed deeply; to fall in love at first sight with this malodorous sleeping girl, with, as far as he could see, no pretentions to beauty or even good looks, was something he had not expected. But falling in love, he had always understood, was unpredictable, and, as far as he was concerned, irrevocable. That they hadn't exchanged a word, nor spoken, made no difference. He, heartwhole until that minute, and with no intention of marrying until it suited him, had lost that same heart.

But he wasn't a callow youth; he would have to tread softly, otherwise he might lose her. He went close to her chair and said gently, 'Miss Holt?'

Sarah opened her eyes and allowed them to travel up a vast expanse of superfine clerical grey cloth, past a richly sombre tie and white linen, until they reached his face.

She said clearly, 'Not Miss Holt; he's my stepfather. Beckwith—Sarah Beckwith. That's a nice tie—Italian silk?'

Mr ter Breukel, aware that she wasn't quite awake

yet, agreed gravely that it was Italian silk. Her eyes, he saw with delight, were quite beautiful, a vivid dark blue, veiled by mousy lashes.

Sarah sat up straight and pushed her hair off her face. 'I'm sorry, I fell asleep.' She studied his face, a very trustworthy face, she decided, as well as a handsome one, with its high-bridged nose and firm mouth and heavy-lidded eyes. 'Mother…?'

'I am Litrik ter Breukel, consultant orthopaedic surgery. I'm sorry there was no one to see you. It has been a busy evening. Your mother is to stay here for a few days. She has been concussed, but should recover quickly. There are one or two cuts and bruises which will heal quickly. Your stepfather has a broken leg, fractured ribs, and he has been cut by glass. He must remain until he is fit to be sent back to England.'

'Do I have to arrange that?'

'No, no. We will see to that at the appropriate time.'

'May I see Mother?'

'Of course. But first I think you must be checked to make sure that you have no injuries. And you will need a tetanus injection and to be cleaned up.'

'I'm not hurt, only dirty and a bit scratched. And I smell dreadful…'

She went without demur to the Accident Room, where he handed her over to a stout, middle-aged woman with a kind face and a harassed manner. She spoke English, too. Sarah submitted to being cleaned up, her scratches and bruises dealt with, her injection given, to the accompaniment of her companion's pleased astonishment that she wasn't more seriously injured, and then, looking clean and smelling of good soap, she was handed back to Mr ter Breukel, who, eyeing her with all the delight of a man in love, thought she looked like some small girl who had been run through the mangle and left to dry.

He said merely, 'You feel better now? We will go to your mother.' And he led the way through the hospital, in and out of lifts, up and down staircases, and eventually into a ward with a dozen beds in it.

Her mother had a corner bed, and was lying back comfortably, but when she saw Sarah she asked peevishly, 'Where have you been? I feel terrible. I'm sure that I'm a good deal worse than these doctors say. You should have been here with me…'

Sarah said gently, 'I'm sorry, Mother. I fell asleep…'

'Asleep? You must have known that I was lying here in pain? And your poor father…'

'Stepfather,' said Sarah.

'Yes, well—it is all very well for you, you don't appear to have been hurt in the least.' She added fretfully, 'I knew this would happen; you always manage to annoy him.'

Sarah said nothing to that, and her mother closed her eyes. 'Now go away and spare a thought for your poor mother before you go to sleep in a comfortable bed.'

Sarah bent and kissed an averted cheek, and then was led away by Mr ter Breukel, who had been standing just behind her, listening to every word.

He made no mention of their conversation, however, but walked her silently to the entrance, where she stopped and offered her hand. 'You've been very kind. Thank you. I know my mother and stepfather will be all right here. May I come and see them in the morning?'

He had no intention of letting her go, and for once a kindly Fate lent a helping hand; Sarah gave a small choking gasp. 'I'm going to be sick...'

There was a providential sink nearby, and she found herself leaning over it, a firm, cool hand holding her head...

Presently she gasped, 'Oh, the relief,' and then, aware of the hand, mumbled, 'How awful for you. I'm so sorry.'

'Best thing you could have done. You probably swallowed a good deal of ditchwater.'

He bent over her, wiped her face with his handkerchief and led her outside into the crisp March evening.

Sarah tugged on an arm to call a halt. 'Thank you,' she said again. 'I'm fine now.'

'You have somewhere to go? Money? Do you know your way about Arnhem?'

She looked away, searching for an answer which wouldn't sound like a fib.

'The police said I could collect our cases and things in the morning from the police station...'

'You know where that is?'

'No, but I can ask.'

'And until morning?' he persisted.

She opened her mouth to utter something misleading but convincing.

'No, no. Let us have no nonsense. You have no

money, no clothes, you are extremely dirty and probably hungry. You will come home with me…'

He spoke pleasantly, but he sounded as though he
meant it. All the same, she said tartly, 'Indeed I
won't.'

Mr ter Breukel slid effortlessly into his bedside
manner. 'My dear young lady, my sister will be delighted to meet you, and help you in any way she
can.' He didn't smile, but Sarah, peeping at him, had
to admit that he looked—she sought the right word—
safe.

'If you're sure I won't be a nuisance, thank you.'

He nodded, walked to where a dark grey Rolls
Royce was parked and popped her neatly into it, got
in beside her and drove away.

After a moment Sarah asked, 'Will I be able to
arrange for Mother to go home soon? If she isn't seriously hurt…'

'Shall we leave that for the moment? Time enough
when you have seen the police in the morning. You
will probably have to make a statement, as will your
parents. Once the matter has been dealt with, arrangements can be made for you to return to England.'

He drove to the city's heart, where there were still
ancient houses and shops which had miraculously es-
caped damage during the terrific battle towards the
end of World War II, stopping presently in a narrow,
canal-lined street.

The houses in it were old, narrow and tall, leaning
against each other, each with a splendid gable. He
stopped the car halfway down, got out and opened
the door for Sarah. She got out and looked around

her. She could have stepped back into the seventeenth
century, for there was no traffic, no cars parked, only
the rustle of trees lining the canal to break the still-
ness.

'You live here?'

'Yes.' He took her arm and marched her across the
narrow pavement and up some worn steps to a handsome door flanked by long narrow windows on either
side of it. He unlocked the door and urged her gently
before him into the narrow hall beyond, its walls panelled, black and white tiles underfoot, a brass chan-
delier, probably as old as the house, hanging from the
beautiful plaster ceiling.

As they entered, a door at the end of the hall
opened, and a short, stout man came to meet them.
He was accompanied by a large dog with small yellow eyes and a thick grey pelt, who bared awesome
teeth in what Sarah hoped was a smile. Apparently it
was, for he pranced up to Mr ter Breukel and offered
his head for a scratch with reassuring meekness.

Mr ter Breukel obliged, exchanged a few words
with the man and switched to English. 'This is Jaap;
he and his wife look after me. And this is Max; he
looks fierce, but he has the disposition of a lamb.'

Sarah shook Jaap's hand, then patted Max's woolly
head and tried not to notice the teeth before she was
propelled gently through a door into a high-ceilinged
room with narrow windows and a hooded fireplace.
She had no time to see more than that before a young
woman got up from a chair by the cheerful fire and
came to meet them.

'Litrik, you're late.' She lifted a face for his kiss and smiled at Sarah.

'Suzanne, this is Sarah Beckwith. She and her parents had a car accident this afternoon. They are at St Bravo's and she has agreed to stay here with us for the night. The police have all their things, and it is rather late to find a hotel…'

Suzanne took Sarah's hand. 'How horrid for you, and we'll love to have you; you must be feeling awful.' She cast a discreet eye over Sarah's deplorable person. 'Would you like a bath before dinner? Anneke can get your clothes cleaned up while I lend you something to wear.'

She took Sarah's arm. 'This is fun—not for you, of course, but I'm so pleased you're here. We'll find Anneke and I'll take you upstairs.'

She turned to her brother. 'Dinner in half an hour? You don't have to go back this evening?'

'No, not unless something turns up.' He gave a casual nod and smile and went to the fire, and Sarah, reassured by the matter-of-fact air he was careful to maintain, went back into the hall and up a carved staircase in a recess halfway down it.

A small, thin woman was waiting for them when they reached the landing.

'This is Anneke,' said Suzanne. 'Jaap's wife and a family friend for years and years.'

Sarah offered a hand once more and was aware that she was being carefully studied from beady brown eyes. Then Anneke smiled and led the way down a passage leading off the landing, opened a door and waved Suzanne and Sarah into the room beyond.

A charming room of pale pastel colours, deeply carpeted, with curtained windows a froth of white muslin. Sarah paused on the threshold. 'My filthy shoes…' She took them off and Anneke took them from her with a smile and said something to Suzanne.

'Take everything off and have a bath. Anneke will see to your things and I'll bring you some clothes.' She studied Sarah's small person. 'We're almost the same size. A sweater and trousers?' She gave Sarah a little push. 'Anneke's running a bath for you; I'll be back in ten minutes.'

Left alone, Sarah shed her damp and dirty clothes, laid them tidily on a towel so as not to spoil the carpet or quilt, and got into the bath. It was blissfully hot and delightfully scented. She could have stayed there for hours, but Suzanne, calling from the open door into the bedroom, roused her.

'I've put some things on the bed. Something is bound to fit, more or less. Dinner in ten minutes.'

Sarah, wrapped in a vast white towel, went to have a look. There was a heap of coloured sweaters, a couple of pairs of trousers, gossamer undies, slippers…

Dressed, her hair still damp and tied back in an untidy plait for lack of ribbons or pins, the trousers on the large side and the pink sweater she had chosen shrouding her person, she took a final look at her reflection. She looked as plain as always, she decided, but at least she was clean and smelling sweet.

She went downstairs and found Jaap in the hall, waiting for her. He led her with a fatherly air back into the drawing room and Mr ter Breukel got up out of his chair and crossed the room with just the right air of a polite host ready to put an unexpected guest at ease.

Suzanne, watching him, hid a smile. Litrik, impervious to the charms of various young ladies that his family, anxious for him to marry, had produced, was showing interest in this nice little creature with the plain face and the lovely eyes. And the pink sweater suited her very well...

Sarah, accepting a chair and a glass of sherry, happily unaware of Suzanne's thoughts, made polite conversation with her host and hostess, and, encouraged by Mr ter Breukel's artless questioning, said that no, she had never been to Arnhem before, had never been in Holland—only her stepfather had wanted to return to England by the night ferry to Harwich.

'Ah, yes—you live somewhere along the east coast? By far the easiest way to return.'

'He has a house near Clapham Common—that's London,' said Sarah flatly. And, since his raised eyebrows invited more than that, added, 'We—that is, Mother and Father, before he died, and me...' She paused. Perhaps it was 'I'. 'We used to live in a small village in Berkshire.'

'Delightful country,' murmured Mr ter Breukel, inviting further confidences.

'Yes, quite different from Clapham Common.'

'You live at home?'

'Yes. Mother isn't very strong...'

Suzanne asked, 'You're not getting married or anything like that?'

'No, we—I don't go out much.'

Mr ter Breukel said easily, 'One never knows what

awaits one round the corner.' He knew, of course, but patience was something of which he had plenty. Having found her, he wasn't going to lose her by being hasty.

Jaap came to tell them that dinner was served; Suzanne took his arm and they crossed the hall to the dining room, with its panelled walls and oval table, the George the First Oak dresser along one wall, the oak Chippendale chairs. A pair of crystal candelabra stood on the dresser, and a silver and cut-glass epergne was at the centre of the table, which was set with lace mats and silverware—very plain, with a crest worn by time.

Sarah gave a quick glance around her and sighed with pleasure. Everything in the room was old and perfect and used—not taken for granted, but neither was it hidden away behind cabinet doors or packed in green baize, to be used only on very special occasions.

The food was good too, simple and beautifully cooked, enhanced by the plates upon which it was served; Delft, she recognised, and old, for they were patterned in pale lavender, not the blue one expected. Washing up would be a hazardous undertaking…

She drank the wine she was offered and Mr ter Breukel watched with satisfaction as the colour came back into her pale face. She hadn't been injured but she had been shocked, although she had done her best to hide that. A good night's sleep, he reflected, and tomorrow he would find the time to consider the future.

*   *   *

Suzanne escorted Sarah to her bed, after a cheerful goodnight from her host.

Sarah got into the silk and lacy nightie Suzanne had found for her and slid into bed, determined to make sensible plans for the morning; once she had retrieved their luggage and money and passports from the police, she reflected, she could decide what was best to be done. She would have to find out just how long her mother and stepfather would have to stay in hospital… That was as far as she got before falling into a refreshing sleep.

She woke to find Anneke standing by the bed with a little tray of tea and holding her clothes, clean and pressed, over one arm. Anneke beamed at her, nodding in response to her good morning, and handed her a note. The writing was a scrawl; it could have been written by a spider dipped in ink. With difficulty Sarah made out that breakfast was at eight o'clock and she would be taken to the hospital directly after the meal. So she smiled and nodded to Anneke, who smiled and nodded in return, before Sarah drank her tea and got out of bed. There wasn't much time; she showered, dressed, did the best she could with her face and hair, and went downstairs.

Mr ter Breukel and Suzanne were already at the table, but he got up to pull out her chair and expressed the hope that she had slept well.

'Very well,' said Sarah. 'Such a pretty room, and the sort of bed you sink into.'

'Good. You had my note?'

She buttered a roll. 'Yes. What shocking hand-writing you have. But I suppose all medical men write badly so that no one can understand, if you see what I mean?'

Suzanne turned a laugh into a cough, and Mr ter Breukel said gravely, 'I think that is very likely.' He gave her a glance just long enough to take in the delightful sight of her in her cleaned and pressed clothes, no make-up and shining mousy hair. Sarah, not seeing the glance, drank her coffee and remarked that he would be wishing to leave for the hospital and she was quite ready when he wished to go.

'Although I'm sure I should be quite all right to walk to the police station. Unless perhaps I should go to the hospital first?'

'Yes, that would be best. Everything depends on the condition of your mother and stepfather.' He got up from the table. 'You'll excuse me? I must telephone. Could you be ready to leave in ten minutes?'

She got into the car beside him presently; she had bidden Suzanne goodbye and thanked her for her kindness, and Suzanne had kissed her cheek, rather to Sarah's surprise, and said it had been fun. Sarah, thinking about it, supposed that for Suzanne it had been just that, and she had liked her... She liked the man sitting beside her too.

At the hospital he nodded a casual goodbye, said that he would see her later, and handed her over to a nurse who took her to her mother.

Mrs Holt was awake and complaining.

'There you are. I hope you'll arrange for us to go back home as quickly as possible. I shall never recover in this place. Tea with no milk, and nothing but thin bread and butter and a boiled egg.'

Sarah bent to kiss her. 'Did you sleep? Do you feel better this morning?'

'Of course I didn't close my eyes all night, and I feel very poorly. Have you got our things yet? I want my own nightgowns; someone must do my hair...'

'I'm going to collect them this morning; I'll bring whatever you need here, Mother.'

'Have you seen your father?'

'Stepfather,' said Sarah. 'No, Nurse tells me that he is to have his leg seen to this morning.'

'How tiresome.' Mrs Holt turned her head away. 'Go and get my things; when you get back I'll tell you if I want anything else.'

Sarah went through the hospital once more and, because she was a kind girl, asked if she could see her stepfather.

He was in a small ward with three other men, and she saw at a glance that he was in no mood to answer her 'good morning'. She stood listening to his diatribe in reply to her enquiry as to how he felt, and, when he had run out of breath, said that she would come and see him after he had had his operation. Only to be told that he couldn't care less if he never saw her again! So she bade him goodbye and started back to the entrance. Neither parent had asked where she had slept or how she felt.

Getting lost on the way out, she had time to think about her future. She supposed that some time during the day someone at the hospital would tell her how long her mother and stepfather would have to remain there. Mr ter Breukel had told her that someone would arrange their return to England, so it seemed best for her to go back as quickly as possible and look after the house until they returned.

She preferred not to think further ahead than that; life hadn't been easy living at home, her sense of duty outweighing her longing to have a life of her own. But her mother, each time Sarah suggested that she might train for something and be independent, had made life unbearable, with her reproaches and sly reminders that her father had told Sarah to look after her mother. Then, of course, he had had no idea that his wife would remarry—and to a man who was in a position to give her a comfortable life. And who had taken a dislike to his stepdaughter the moment they had met.

She found the main entrance at last, but halfway to it she was stopped.

A porter addressed her in surprisingly good English. She was to wait—he indicated an open doorway beyond which people were sitting.

Perhaps she was to be told what arrangements had been made for her parents. She sat down obediently; there was no point in getting fussed. She had hoped to return to England that day, but probably she would have to spend another night in Arnhem. Which should hold no terrors for her; she would have some money once she had been to the police station, and all she had to do was wait for someone to tell her what to do next.

There were a great many posters on the walls, and she was making futile guesses as to what they were about when the porter tapped her on the shoulder.

She followed him back to the entrance hall and saw

Mr ter Breukel standing by the doors. Her smile at the sight of him—filled with relief and delight—shook him badly, but all he said was 'I'll take you to the police station,' with detached courtesy.

CHAPTER TWO

'CAN you spare the time?' asked Sarah anxiously. 'Don't you have patients to see?'

'I have already seen them.' Mr ter Breukel was at his most soothing. 'I shall be operating this afternoon. On your stepfather, amongst others.'

'How soon will I know when he can go home?'

'Probably later this evening. Ah, here is the police station.'

She was glad that he was with her. She gave a succinct account of the accident, and from time to time he was a great help translating some tricky word the officer hadn't understood. All the same it took a long time, and after that the luggage had to be checked, money counted, passports examined. She was given hers, as well as some money from her stepfather's wallet. He wouldn't like that, she reflected, signing for it, but she would need money to get back home. And supposing her mother travelled with her?

She explained that to Mr ter Breukel and waited for his advice.

'Does your mother have traveller's cheques in her handbag?'

The handbag was an expensive one from one of the big fashion houses, unlike Sarah's own rather shabby leather shoulder bag, and there *were* traveller's cheques inside, and quite a lot of money.

'Good. You can give the bag to your mother and she can arrange for it to be kept in safe-keeping until she leaves.'

Put like that, it all sounded very simple. But they went back to St Bravo's and suddenly nothing was simple any more.

Her mother's X-ray had shown a hairline fracture; there was no question of her leaving the hospital for some time. And there was no time to talk about it, for Mr ter Breukel had been called away the moment they arrived back.

Sarah unpacked what she thought her mother might need, and when that lady demanded her handbag gave it to her. Then she went in search of the ward sister, who told her kindly enough that it would be most unwise for her mother to be moved. 'And, since your father must stay also, they can return together when they are able to travel.'

Sarah went to see the other ward sister about her stepfather then. He was already in Theatre, and Mr ter Breukel was operating. 'Come back later, about six o'clock, and we will tell you what has been done.'

So Sarah went out of the hospital and into the main streets. The luggage was safe with a porter, she had money in her pocket and she was hungry.

She found a small café and sat over coffee and a roll filled with cheese, deciding what she should do next. It made sense to find a tourist information office and find out about getting back home. Maybe not for a few days, but she would need to know...

It wasn't difficult to find, so she went inside and found that the girls behind the counter spoke English. She could fly, they told her, an easy train ride to the airport at Schiphol, or she could get a ferry from the Hoek van Holland or from Scheveningen to Harwich. They could arrange it for her.

Sarah thanked them, then asked if they knew of a small, inexpensive hotel. They went to a lot of trouble, and she left presently with a short list from which to choose. Now it was just a question of going back to St Bravo's, finding out about her stepfather, seeing her mother, collecting her case from the porter and moving into whichever hotel had a room vacant.

She went into another café and had a cup of tea and some biscuits, and then found her way back to the hospital. She went first to see her stepfather, who was nicely recovered from the anaesthetic but whose temper was uncertain. He was propped up on his pillows, a leg in plaster under a cradle. In reply to her civil and sympathetic enquiry as to how he felt, he said angrily, 'That infernal surgeon says that I must remain here for at least two weeks...'   .

'I thought that once the plaster was dry you could walk with a crutch...'

'Don't be a fool. A broken rib has pierced my lung; it has to heal before I'm fit to be moved.'

'Oh—oh, I'm sorry. I'll tell Mother. I'm going to see her now.'

'And don't bother to come and see me. The less I see of you the better—if it hadn't been for you…'

No doubt he had told anyone who would listen that it had been her fault. She bade him goodbye and went along to see her mother.

That lady was sitting up in bed, pecking at her supper.

'It's so early,' she complained, as soon as she set eyes on Sarah. 'How can I possibly eat at half past six in the evening?'

Sarah sat down by the bed and listened with outward patience to her parent's grumbles. When there was a pause, she told her about her stepfather.

'How tiresome. What is to happen to me, I should like to know? I've no intention of staying here a day longer than I must. You will have to take me home, Sarah. Your father—' she caught Sarah's eye '—stepfather can return when he's recovered. I can't be expected to look after him. Of course *you* will be at home, but I suppose you will need some help.'

She didn't ask Sarah how she had spent her day—Sarah hadn't expected her to—but told her to come the next morning.

'You must get me that special night-cream—and a paler lipstick, oh, and a bed jacket. Pink, something pretty. I don't see why I should look dowdy just because I am in this horrible place.'

'Mother,' said Sarah, 'this is a splendid hospital, and if you hadn't been brought here you might be feeling a lot worse.'

Mrs Holt squeezed out a tear. 'How hard-hearted you are, Sarah. Go away and enjoy yourself—and don't be late here in the morning. I want that bed jacket before the doctors do their rounds.'

Sarah stifled a wish to burst into tears; she was tired and hungry by now, and the future loomed ahead in a most unsatisfactory manner. She bade her mother goodnight and went in search of Sister.

Her mother was doing well, she was told; rather excitable and unco-operative, but that was to be expected with concussion. Sarah could rest assured that hospital was the best place for her mother for the moment, and that as soon as possible she and Mr Holt would be transferred back home.

'So you need have no more worries,' said Sister kindly.

Sarah began the lengthy walk back to the entrance. She must get her case and then go to one of the hotels. She had spent rather longer that she had meant to with her mother, and somewhere a clock chimed seven. She hadn't been looking where she was going and had got lost again. She stood in the long corridor, wondering if she should go to the left or the right...

A hand on her arm swept her straight ahead. 'Lost?' asked Mr ter Breukel cheerfully. 'We'll collect your case and go home. Suzanne will be wondering where we are.'

Sarah, trotting to keep up, and aware that everything was suddenly all right again, said, 'Well, thank you very much, but I'm going to a hotel. I went to something called VVV and they gave me a list...'

Mr ter Breukel stopped so suddenly that she almost fell over. 'Did I not tell you this morning that you would be staying with us until we know more about your parents? You must forgive me; I have a shocking memory.'

'No, you didn't say anything.' She gave him a thoughtful look. 'You can't have a bad memory; surgeons must have excellent memories, otherwise they would put things back in the wrong place!'

'That is a terrifying thought,' said Mr ter Breukel, grave-faced, and he hurried her along to the entrance. He found a porter to fetch her case, opened his car door, ushered her in and got in beside her.

'The hotel,' said Sarah. 'I mean, I can't impose upon your kindness, really, I can't.'

He said briskly, 'I must tell you about your stepfather, give you some idea of how long he will be with us—and your mother, too. I'm a busy man during the day, so our only chance to discuss this is in the evening. You do agree?'

'Well, yes…'

'Good. Are you hungry?'

'Famished,' said Sarah, without thinking, and then very quickly added, 'I had something to eat in a café.'

'Where?'

'I'm not sure exactly. It said "Snack Bar" over the door.'

'A roll and cheese and a cup of coffee?' He added gently, 'Sarah, you don't need to pretend with me.'

She realised with contented relief that he meant what he said. 'I know that, and I promise I won't do that. I *am* famished.'

Mr ter Breukel's handsome features remained impassive. A step in the right direction, he reflected. He cast a quick glance at her profile, which she didn't see. Her small nose had a slight tilt to it—most endearing...

What happy chance, reflected Sarah, had led them to meet again like this?

Mr ter Breukel could have told her, of course, but he didn't intend to. He had his own methods of getting information about visitors, and an intimate knowledge of the many corridors of St Bravo's helped.

Suzanne came to meet them as they entered the house. 'Oh, good, you're punctual. Oh, and you've got your case, Sarah. Jaap will take it up to your room, but don't bother to unpack it till later. Come and have a drink before dinner.'

Sarah, rather overwhelmed by this ready welcoming—just as though she had been expected to return, she thought—followed Jaap and her case upstairs and, despite Suzanne's invitation to go straight back down again and have a drink, fished around in her case and found the jersey dress she intended to wear. It was an unpretentious garment, in an inoffensive blue, and she didn't like it much, but it could be rolled up small and stuffed into her case and didn't crease.

She put it on quickly and tidied her hair, did her face rather carelessly and went back downstairs. She would have liked time to make the best of herself—she supposed Mr ter Breukel had that effect on any girl—but she was only here in his house so that he could tell her if any arrangements should be made for her mother and stepfather's return to England...

She accepted a glass of sherry, gave Suzanne an account of her day when she was pressed to do so, glossing over the bits that had been dull, and then ate her dinner, making polite conversation—the weather, the amazing ability of everyone in Arnhem to speak English, the delicious coffee.

Mr ter Breukel listened to her pretty voice, entranced; as far as he was concerned she could recite the multiplication tables and he would find it exciting. He made suitable replies in a voice of impersonal friendliness, and only as they were drinking their coffee in the drawing room did he begin to tell her about her parents.

They were sitting round the fireplace, she and Suzanne on the vast sofa facing it, he in a great wing-back chair with Max lying over his feet. The room looked beautiful, the soft light from the table lamps showing up the magnificent bow-fronted cabinets with their displays of silver and porcelain, casting shadows on the heavy velvet curtains, and yet, despite the magnificence of its contents, the room was welcoming and lived in. And Mr ter Breukel was exactly right for it, thought Sarah; he fitted the room and the room fitted him.

You're letting your imagination run away with you, Sarah told herself silently, and sat up straight because he had put down his coffee cup and saucer and now said briskly, 'Let me tell you what has been done today—your mother is comfortable, but she is, if you will forgive me for saying so, not an easy patient. She wishes to go back to England, naturally enough, but I can't advise that. She needs rest and quiet and to have time to resume her normal outlook on life; I have explained to her that once she is home with your stepfather she will need to feel fit herself.

'I operated on him this afternoon; he has quite a severe fracture of the tibia, which I have put together and put in plaster. He will be got up within a few days, but there's no question of him using the leg for weeks. He will be given crutches, but he is a heavy man and not very co-operative. So I think that their return to England must be ruled out for two weeks at least. Arrangements must be made so that they can travel easily, and there must be some kind of nursing aid at your home. Your mother tells me that she would be quite unable to do that. He'll need physiotherapy, and of course the plaster will probably need renewing later on.'

He paused, but Sarah didn't say anything. She was thinking with despair of the weeks ahead, at the beck and call of her stepfather, who would expect her to fulfil the duties of nurse as well as the major tasks of the household. There was a housekeeper, and help for the heavy chores, but there would be the shopping and the ironing and the endless jobs her mother would want done… I mustn't moan, reflected Sarah.

'So I had better go home as quickly as possible and get things arranged.' She thought for a moment. 'I'd have to come back when they're ready to return—to help Mother.'

'That is, of course, one solution.' Mr ter Breukel gave the impression of someone giving friendly advice. 'But I wonder if you have given thought to remaining here and returning with your parents? It so happens that I might be able to offer an alternative solution.

'We have a great-aunt, living in Arnhem, whose companion has had to return to her home to nurse her mother; she may be away for several weeks. You might take over her duties until your parents are ready to leave the hospital. It is probably a job you wouldn't care to undertake—rather dull and needing a good deal of patience. On the other hand, you would have a roof over your head, be able to visit your mother and be here when they are ready to leave.'

'What a splendid idea,' declared Suzanne. She had visited her aunt that very afternoon and her companion, Juffrouw Telle, had been there. Moreover there had been no question of her going home. But Suzanne had no doubt that if Litrik said that Juffrouw Telle was going to nurse her sick mother, then he had contrived something for his own ends. Sarah, thought Suzanne with satisfaction, had done something none of the other women acquaintances in whom he had shown no interest had been able to do—she had stolen his heart.

Suzanne said encouragingly to Sarah, 'Do think about that, Sarah. Great-Aunt is quite an old dear, and you would be able to see your mother every day. I'm sure she would miss you terribly if you went back to England.'

Sarah said, 'Your aunt—great-aunt—might not like me... Besides, her companion might not be ready to return when Mother and my stepfather leave.' She added, 'Or she might come back within the next few days.'

'Unlikely. Her mother will need nursing for ten days at least,' improvised Mr ter Breukel smoothly, 'and if you should have to leave before she returns, then we shall have to find someone else. In the meantime you would be helping several people, and I for one would be most grateful.'

Which reminded Sarah that this was a way in which she could repay him for his kindness. And there was no denying that it was a way out of her problem.

Mr ter Breukel, watching her face, was delighted to see that his plotting and planning were likely to be successful. He reminded himself that he must find a suitable gift for Juffrouw Telle. Middle-aged, patient and kind-hearted, she had been with his great-aunt for years; she was almost one of the family, and had been only too ready to agree to his scheme. It gave her an unexpected holiday, and the pleasure of sharing a secret which held more than a whiff of romance…

Sarah didn't waste time weighing up the pros and cons; the pros were obvious, and if there were any cons she would deal with them later. She said, 'Thank you, I would be glad to help out until your aunt's companion is able to return. And it is I who should be grateful, for now I don't need to worry about anything.'

For the next week or two, at any rate, she added silently. And after that I'll think of something.

Suzanne said, 'Oh, splendid. I'll take you to Great-Aunt tomorrow. In the afternoon? You'll want to see your mother and stepfather first.'

Sarah thanked her, stifling the wish that Mr ter Breukel had offered to take her, reminding herself that he was a busy man and had wasted enough of his time on her anyway.

Her stepfather showed no pleasure at the sight of her, and, apprised of her plans, merely grunted. 'Do what you please, as long as you're back here to look after your mother when we go home. And that can't be soon enough.' He began a tirade against the nurses, the doctors, the food, and the fact that there was no private room available for him. Sarah, having heard it all before, listened patiently and assured him that he would be able to go home the moment he was allowed to, and then she slipped away. It seemed to her that the hospital staff would be only too glad to see the back of him.

Her mother was sitting in the Day Room, reading a magazine, and she greeted Sarah peevishly.

'Should you be reading?' asked Sarah.

'No, but the nurses don't come in here very often, and when they do I hide it under a cushion.' Mrs Holt allowed her mouth to droop. 'I have such a headache.'

'That's because you're reading.'

'Well, I'm bored. I want to go home…'

'I dare say it won't be much longer. Mother, I've got a job. Not paid, of course, but being a companion to an old lady while her usual companion goes home to look after her mother. I may stay there until we go back home.'

'Trust you to find a comfortable place to live while I have to stay in this dreary place.'

Sarah supposed that the concussion had made her mother so difficult. 'It's not so bad, Mother. I expect I'll be able to come and see you quite often.'

'When you do, bring me some nail varnish. Elizabeth Arden, pink—at least I can give myself a manicure.' Mrs Holt closed her eyes. 'I do have a headache…'

Sarah kissed her and left the hospital. On the way out she caught a glimpse of Mr ter Breukel, enormous even at a distance, surrounded by white-coated satellites. He didn't see her, but the sight of him cheered her up as she walked back to his house.

He had, in fact, turned his head in time to see her disappearing down one of the endless corridors. He would have liked to have taken her himself to his great-aunt's house, but to display too much interest might frighten her off…

Sarah got into Suzanne's car after they had had coffee and was driven into the centre of the city to another old gabled house in a quiet street close to the Grote Kerk. Suzanne didn't give Sarah time to feel nervous. She urged her out of the car, thumped the massive door-knocker and they were admitted before Sarah could draw breath.

The old man who opened the door looked shaky on his legs. He had white hair and pale blue eyes in a wrinkled face. Suzanne threw her arms around him and kissed his cheek, and said something to make him chuckle before she turned to Sarah.

'Kaes has been with Great-Aunt for almost the whole of his life. He's part of the house.' She spoke to him again, and Sarah held out a hand and smiled at the friendly old man. He studied her for a moment and then led them down the hall to double doors on one side of it, opened them, said something to the room's occupant and trotted off.

Suzanne gave Sarah a friendly shove, and Sarah found herself crossing a vast expanse of carpet to the very old lady sitting in a high-backed chair by one of the tall windows.

Suzanne skipped to her side, kissed her and spoke rapidly in Dutch, and then switched to English.

'This is Sarah Beckwith, Tante, come to keep you company until Juffrouw Telle gets back. She can't speak a word of Dutch, but that won't matter, will it? She will be able to read your English novels. You like being read to, don't you?'

The little old lady spoke. She had a soft voice, but now it had a slight edge to it. 'Suzanne, don't mumble. Where is this young woman who is to stay with me until Anna Telle returns? If she mumbles she will be of no use to me.'

Suzanne beckoned Sarah. 'She's here, Tante.'

Sarah stood quietly while she was studied through a pair of lorgnettes, and then took the small be-ringed hand and shook it gently. She said clearly, 'How do you do, *Mevrouw*? I hope I shall be of use to you until Juffrouw Telle returns. I am sorry I can't speak Dutch…'

'No matter, just as long as you speak your own language clearly. Suzanne, ring the bell, Reneke shall take Miss Beckwith to her room. We will have lunch together in half an hour.'

Which meant, reflected Sarah, that she was to go to her room and return in half an hour. She followed a stout, placid woman up the staircase at the end of the hall and into a room at the front of the house. It was large, and the furniture in it was solid. It was comfortable, too, and there were flowers in a little vase on the massive dressing table. There was a bathroom across the passage, as old-fashioned as the room, but equipped with modern comforts. The bath, thought Sarah, eyeing its size, in the middle of the room, balanced on its four iron feet, had been installed for a giant. Her thoughts wandered for a moment; Mr ter Breukel was a giant, and a very nice one...

She unpacked, tidied her person, examined her face in the oval mirror and wished for good looks, applied discreet lipstick and then went to look out of the window. It was tall and wide and gave her an excellent view of the street below and the buildings around it, with the Grote Kerk towering at its end. It was quiet there, but at the other end of the street she could see a busy thoroughfare and the glint of water. She would have to discover the best way to reach the hospital, but just for the moment the hospital, her mother, and all the adherent problems seemed blessedly far away.

She left the window. Like many old houses, this

one was peaceful, and people had been happy living in it, just as she had felt at Mr ter Breukel's home.

She wandered round the room, looking at the few pictures on its wall, picking up ornaments and putting them down again. She hoped that she would see Mr ter Breukel again, for she liked him. She examined a small porcelain figure on the bedside table, a charming trifle probably worth a small fortune. She was thinking too much about him and that wouldn't do. He had been kind, but he was a man to be kind— to an old woman crossing the street, or to a lost dog. Probably he would forget all about her now that she was dealt with—a problem solved...

The half-hour was up; she went back to the room where the old lady and Suzanne were waiting.

'After lunch, when Suzanne has gone, I will explain your duties to you,' said her hostess. 'They are, I believe, not onerous. You will be able to visit your mother at St Bravo's. I am sure that we shall get on well together.'

They had their lunch in a sombre room panelled in some dark wood, sitting at a table which would seat ten perfectly comfortably. It was a simple meal, beautifully served, and Sarah, who had been dreading it, found that she was enjoying herself. Old Mevrouw ter Breukel might be getting on in years, but there was nothing wrong with her brain. She was as sharp as a needle: up to date with politics, fashion and the latest books.

Presently wishing Suzanne goodbye, Sarah assured her that she was going to be happy in her unexpected job. 'I'll do my best to please your aunt,' she said. 'You've been so kind, and so has Mr ter Breukel. Thank you both very much. I'll let you know when I'm going back to England.'

'Do, though I'll probably see you before then. I hope you won't find it too dull.'

Sarah thought of the uneventful life she led at home. 'It's the most exciting thing that's happened to me in years.'

Her duties were indeed light: she was to spend a good deal of the day with Mevrouw ter Breukel, reading, writing letters for her, fetching and carrying such odds and ends as the lady wanted, and making sure that she was comfortable and lacked for nothing. In the afternoon she was to have an hour or so free, and there would be plenty of time to go and see her mother.

Once her duties had been made known to her she was bidden to fetch a book and read aloud until the old lady had her afternoon nap.

The book took Sarah by surprise. It was the latest Ruth Rendell.

'Juffrouw Telle doesn't read English well, and it tires me to read. We will read as many books as possible while you are here,' said Mevrouw ter Breukel surprisingly. 'Litrik keeps me supplied with the books I enjoy—Jack Higgins, P.D. James, Evelyn Anthony, Freeling. Sit there, child, I hear better on this side. I'm halfway through the book—there's a bookmark.'

Sarah found the place and started to read. She had a pleasant voice and the story was exciting; it kept them both absorbed until an elderly woman brought in the tea tray.

'No milk, no sugar,' commanded the old lady, 'and I'll have a biscuit.'

Sarah drank her tea from a paper-thin cup and answered the questions which Mevrouw ter Breukel fired at her in a soft voice. No, she didn't have a young man, nor had she any prospect of marrying one, and, no, she didn't have a job. Her life, outlined for the old lady's benefit, sounded dull in her ears.

They dined later, the two of them, in the dark grandeur of the dining room, and Sarah was glad that she had changed into the blue jersey, for Mevrouw ter Breukel was wearing black taffeta and diamonds.

Told, kindly enough, to go to bed soon after the *stoel* clock struck ten, Sarah went willingly. She wasn't tired, but the old lady had observed that occasionally, when she was unable to sleep, she expected someone to keep her company during the wakeful hours. But nothing happened to disturb Sarah's sleep.

She was up and dressed by eight o'clock and had gone, as she had been told, to Mevrouw ter Breukel's room, to find that old lady sitting up in a vast bed, a four-poster, doing a jigsaw puzzle.

They exchanged good mornings and Sarah spent five minutes picking up bits of the puzzle which had been flung aside before she was told to go and have her breakfast.

'And bring me my letters in half an hour or so. Then I shall not need you for a hour or more. Go to the hospital, if you wish, and enquire about your parents. Kaes will look after you and tell you how to get to St Bravo's.'

Dismissed, Sarah went downstairs and found Kaes waiting for her. Her breakfast had been laid with great elegance in a small room behind the dining room, and she enjoyed every morsel of it, keeping an eye on the clock. Half an hour later she went back with the post, and found Mevrouw ter Breukel still engrossed in her puzzle.

'Run along now, and be back here by half past ten.'

The hospital was ten minutes' walk away, and there were several ambulances parked by the Accident Room entrance. She went up to her mother's ward and met Sister coming out of the office.

'You have come to see your mother? She has slept well; she will be glad to see you. We are busy today. There has been a multiple car accident, and soon we shall have more patients here.'

Mrs Holt was sitting by a window. 'You must do some shopping for me,' she began, without preamble. 'I need some more mascara and another lipstick, and see if you can get me a decent magazine; I've nothing to read…'

'Don't they come round with books? I'm sure they'd find you something in English, Mother.'

'Oh, yes, but you know how quickly reading bores me.'

'TV?'

'In Dutch, my dear? You must be joking. I'm to

see the consultant this morning. I shall ask to go home.'

'What about my stepfather?'

'Oh, they will arrange to send him home, too, of course. He must be able to travel by now.'

'Have you been to see him?'

'My dear Sarah, I'm not well; my nerves wouldn't stand it. Sister tells me from time to time how he is. You had better go and see him.'

Sarah went, unwillingly enough, but she saw it as her duty. It was a waste of time, of course. Her stepfather did not wish to see her. Her visit was brief and she soon made her way back to the entrance, hoping that she might meet Mr ter Breukel; he would be too busy to stop and talk, but it would be nice just to say hello.

They met on a staircase. She was going down as he was going up, two steps at a time, followed by two younger men in long white coats. He didn't pause; she doubted if he had seen her.

He had, of course, but sudden emergencies took no account of personal feelings.

Sarah had the good sense to see that she had probably been invisible to him; he was so obviously involved in some dire situation. He had looked different, too, and she realised why. He had been wearing grey trousers and a high-necked pullover, and he hadn't shaved. Perhaps he had been up half the night.

The whole night, actually.

There was no time to shop for her mother, and she hurried back to Mevrouw ter Breukel, anxious not to be late.

The day went smoothly and pleasantly enough, and, to her surprise, quickly. She was kept busy, and when the old lady discovered that she could play chess, after a fashion, the evening hours were fully occupied. Sarah went to bed at length, feeling that the day had gone well. Only it would have been nice if Mr ter Breukel had called to see his aunt.

A wish, had she but known it, which he would have heartily endorsed.

But he came the next day. It was the quiet hour or so after tea, and Sarah was setting out the chess pieces, ready for a game after dinner, her neat head bent over the chessboard. He stood in the open doorway, watching her, studying her small person, wanting very much to go to her and gather her into his arms and tell her that he loved her. But not just yet, he warned himself, and went into the room.

His great-aunt was clearly taking a nap. Sarah turned round and saw him and smiled and put her finger to her lips. He smiled back, took her arm and led her to the far end of the room by the window. Only then did he say, 'Hello, Sarah.'

She beamed up at him. 'Hello. Mevrouw ter Breukel will wake presently. Do you want tea or anything?'

'Nothing, thank you. Have you settled down? Not too hard work?'

'I'm very happy, and it isn't like work at all. Your great-aunt is a darling old lady.' She spoke in a whisper, and, when he didn't answer, asked, 'Have you been busy? There were a lot of ambulances when I went to see Mother yesterday.'

'A day of emergencies.'

'I—I saw you yesterday—you didn't see me. It was on the stairs. You looked as though you have been up all night.'

'It was a night of emergencies, too. Sarah, before you return to England, I should like to show you something of Holland. I shall be free on Sunday, will you spend it with me?'

'With you? You mean all day?' The delight in her face changed to regret. 'But I can't; I'm here to be your aunt's companion.'

'But like all companions you are entitled to a free day each week. Besides, Suzanne is coming to spend the day here, and you won't be needed.'

When she would have protested, he added casually, 'I think we might enjoy each other's company.'

'Yes, well—but there must be other people—I mean friends you'd rather be with.'

'They are always here. You will go home shortly, and I think that you deserve at least a brief glimpse of Holland!'

'Well, thank you. I would like it very much.' And, Sarah being Sarah, she added, 'I'm afraid I'm not a very interesting person to be with. I mean, I'm not clever or witty. You might get bored...'

Mr ter Breukel's expression of calm interest didn't alter. 'After the rush and hurry of St Bravo's I dare say I shall find your company restful. Shall we say nine o'clock on Sunday morning?'

'All right. But I must ask Mevrouw ter Breukel's permission.'

She was interrupted by that lady's voice demanding to know what they were talking about, and when she was told she observed that it suited her very well. 'For if Suzanne is to spend the day with me I'll not need Sarah here as well. Take her through the Veluwe, Litrik, and show her how lovely it is there.'

She offered a cheek for his kiss. 'Sarah, go for a walk, or amuse yourself for half an hour or so. We will have our game of chess after dinner.'

When Sarah had gone, and he had shut the door behind her, she said, 'Litrik, I may be an old woman but I still have my wits about me. You're in love with the girl, aren't you?'

He came and sat down opposite to her, speaking Dutch now. 'Yes, my dear. I knew that the moment I set eyes on her.'

'But she has no idea of that. Only she likes you very much indeed, I think.'

'Perhaps I am too old for her.'

'That's not going to stop you...'

Mr ter Breukel laughed. 'No, it's not!'

CHAPTER THREE

SARAH woke on Sunday to a fine spring morning. True, the sky was a very pale blue and held no warmth, but the tiled roofs of the houses around her sparkled and the air, when she leaned out of the window, was fresh.

At nine o'clock precisely she was borne away in the discreet luxury of Mr ter Breukel's Rolls, unaware of her companion's delight at her company since he had greeted her with casual friendliness and now began almost immediately to describe the various parts of Arnhem as he drove out of the city: the war memorial at the Rhine Bridge, the parks, the old houses which had survived the destruction of the War, the zoo.

Sarah craned her neck from side to side, anxious not to miss anything.

He drove north presently, through the High Veluwe national park, taking the narrow by-roads through the woods and stopping for coffee in Apeldoorn, where he walked her to the palace of Het Loo.

The park was open and they wandered to and fro, explored the stable block, which was open to the public, and then got back into the car to drive on to Zwolle. Here they lunched at a small restaurant housed in an ancient house by the Stads Gracht, once a moat and now a canal, and were served *koffietafel*—

a basket of various rolls and bread and slices of cheese on a vast platter, cold meat and sausage, hard-boiled eggs and a salad, accompanied by a pot of coffee.

Sarah eyed the table with pleasure; the morning's sightseeing and her pleasure in her companion's company had given her an appetite, moreover she felt happy. Somehow in Mr ter Breukel's placid company the future became vague and unthreatening.

They travelled on presently, through Meppel and into Friesland, to stop for tea in Sneek, and then had a brief glimpse of the lake before driving on to the coast. It was chilly here, and the North Sea looked grey and forbidding.

'Lovely in the summer,' Mr ter Breukel told her. 'Those islands you can see are popular with families. There are splendid beaches for children. You like children?'

Sarah was unaware of how wistful she looked. 'Oh, yes…'

Children, she thought, and dogs and cats and a don-key, and an old house with a huge garden—and a husband, of course. And what chance had she of get-ting any of them? The future, so pleasantly vague, suddenly became only too real.

Mr ter Breukel took her arm and walked her back to the car. In some way his hand on hers dispelled her gloomy thoughts. The future didn't matter, not for the moment at any rate.

He drove back over the Afsluitdijk, gave her a glimpse of Alkmaar and raced south, bypassing Am-sterdam. 'You shall see that another time,' he told her casually. 'There's rather a nice place where we can have dinner just outside Utrecht.'

The 'nice place' was a seventeenth-century mansion, very splendid, overlooking a pond and tucked away in the centre of a small wood. Sarah, led away to a well-equipped cloakroom, did her hair and face, wishing for chestnut curls and a pretty face as she did so, wishing too that she was wearing a smart outfit worthy of her companion and her surroundings. She told herself in her sensible way not to be silly, and joined Mr ter Breukel in a large, rather old-fashioned lounge to sip her sherry while they discussed what they should eat.

Sarah, with gentle prompting from Mr ter Breukel, chose tiny pancakes filled with goat's cheese, sole served with a champagne sauce, and chocolate and almond pudding. She ate with a splendid appetite, her tongue nicely loosened by the white wine he had chosen, so that by seemingly casual questions he was made the recipient of a good deal of information concerning her life at Clapham Common. Not that she complained about it; it was what she *didn't* say that gave him an insight into its dullness. He was impatient to rescue her at once, but that, of course, was impossible. He must rely on a kindly Fate and his own plans.

Sarah looked up and caught his eye and smiled, and he schooled his features into a friendly glance and made a casual remark about their surroundings. He wondered what the surrounding diners would do if he were to swoop across the table and pick Sarah up and carry her off. Somewhere quiet, where he

could kiss her at leisure. He smiled then, and Sarah
said, 'Oh, it's lovely here. I shall remember it all
when I get back home.'

'Good. You have only seen a small part of Holland,
though.'

And all she was likely to see, thought Sarah. He
hadn't suggested that he would take her out again,
and she hadn't expected him to. But supposing he
thought that she had hoped he *would*. She had done
her best to be good company, but probably he had
found her rather dull, and after all he had been more
than kind.

Suzanne was still at the house when they got back.

'I've helped Great-Aunt to bed,' she told them.
'We've had a lovely day, gossiping and playing back-
gammon. Did you two enjoy yourselves?'

Her brother said gravely that for his part he had
had a most interesting day, which Sarah considered
was neither one thing or the other.

'It was lovely,' she told Suzanne. 'I'll have so
much to remember when I get back home.'

She bade them goodnight presently, before they
drove away, and then went to her room and went to
bed, remembering every minute of the day. Mr ter
Breukel hadn't said anything about seeing her again,
but of course they were bound to meet, even if it were
only to make arrangements for her mother and stepfather's return to England. Besides, she reminded herself, he visited his great-aunt frequently.

But there was no sign of him. She had caught the
occasional glimpse of him in the distance when she

had visited her mother at the hospital, but he'd been so far away that only the size and height of him had made her sure that it was he. Certainly he didn't visit his great-aunt again, nor were there any messages concerning the transfer to England of her mother.

Mrs Holt, while still complaining bitterly, had settled down at last to the quiet routine of the hospital, and Sister had assured Sarah that she should be fit to return home very shortly. And her stepfather, although one of the worst patients the ward sister assured Sarah that she had ever had to nurse, was fit to travel.

'You will be told when arrangements have been made,' she said to Sarah kindly.

The best part of a week went by; there was no news of Juffrouw Telle's return, and when Sarah saw Suzanne, which was frequently, that young lady professed to know nothing.

It was on an early morning, when Sarah went down to her breakfast after peeping in to see if the old lady was still sleeping, that she found Mr ter Breukel sitting at the table in the small room where she took her meals when she was alone. Everything necessary for a good breakfast was arranged around him, and a folded newspaper was beside his plate.

Sarah paused in the doorway, delighted to see him but not sure if she was welcome. She said, 'Hello,' and then, more sedately, 'Good morning, Mr ter Breukel.'

He had got to his feet and pulled out a chair, and she saw that he was wearing a grey sweater and corduroy trousers. 'You've been up all night,' she observed, and indeed he looked tired; he had showered, but there were lines in his face which she hadn't seen before. 'I hope you will go straight to bed when you've had your breakfast.'

Mr ter Breukel, who had other plans, said that yes, he would, in a meek voice, and pushed the coffee pot towards her.

Sarah said in her practical way, 'Shouldn't you be at your own home?'

He had forgotten how tired he was; he looked into the future and saw with deep satisfaction homecomings in the small hours to Sarah's wifely concern.

'Indeed I should, but it seemed a good opportunity to see you about your mother and stepfather's transfer to England. It has been arranged for Tuesday—that gives you three days to carry out any plans you may have made. Your stepfather will need to travel by ambulance, and your mother can go with him. You will fly from Schiphol and an ambulance will collect you at Heathrow and get you home to Clapham. You will be travelling with them, of course. Someone will come for you on Tuesday morning at eight o'clock.'

Sarah didn't speak for a bit; she was battling with the sudden fright that she wasn't going to see him again. She choked it down and said gruffly, 'Thank you for making all the arrangements; we're very much in your debt. We're very grateful.' Well, *she* was; she wasn't sure about her mother and stepfather. 'I'll be ready, and if there's anything I should do, will someone let me know? And what about your great-aunt? I've loved being with her, and she does need someone, you know…'

Mr ter Breukel buttered a roll lavishly. 'It is amazing how things arrange themselves,' he observed blandly. 'Juffrouw Telle phoned last night to say that she would be returning on Monday evening.'

'Her mother's better? I'm glad, and how provi…'

'…dential,' finished Mr ter Breukel. 'Great-Aunt has enjoyed your company and you have been a great help to us. I'm only sorry you haven't had more time to see Holland.'

'I had a lovely day with you,' said Sarah. 'I shall remember it always.' She added hastily, in case he thought she meant him and his company, 'The country was delightful.'

He kept a straight face while he watched the colour wash over her cheeks. To have accompanied her to England would have been a delight, but he had decided against. First let her return to her own home; there was always the possibility that, viewed from the other side of the North Sea, their growing friendship might dwindle into a vague interlude. That was something he would have to discover later.

He smiled gently. 'Yes, it was a delightful day.' And five minutes later he was leaving, with the casual remark that he would see her before she left Arnhem.

'And go to bed—just for an hour or two,' said Sarah, in such a concerned voice that he was tempted to pick her up and kiss her. But he didn't, and bed, as far as he could see, was something to be deferred until he had dealt with his patients. So he smiled, patted her on a shoulder and was gone.

Sarah, visiting her mother later that day, found her in a state of excitement and with numerous requests to Sarah which she hadn't a hope of fulfilling. She pointed out that once they were home her mother could buy the things she declared she must have, that there was no need to be made up, have her hair done or send Sarah to buy the host of small unnecessary articles she required.

'Of course you *would* say that,' declared Mrs Holt crossly. 'The smallest thing I ask you to do for me and you have a reason for not doing it.'

She turned a shoulder to Sarah. 'You had better go and see your stepfather and see if he needs anything. And you're not to leave me on the journey. I feel ill at the very thought of it.'

Come to think of it, thought Sarah, I feel ill too…

Her stepfather did nothing to improve matters; he queried and argued about every arrangement made for his transfer, and grumbled that his car, which had been transported back to Clapham, was no doubt damaged beyond repair and that no one had seen fit to give him any information about it. He grumbled, too, at the expense of the ambulance, the special arrangements which had been made at the airports—indeed there was nothing about which he *didn't* grumble!

And Sarah made it worse by asking him for money to buy a thank-you gift for the nursing staff. She waited stoically while he vented his rage at the very idea, and then said, 'I should think about a hundred *gulden* would do—for a really handsome box of chocolates they can share around.'

There was no sign of Mr ter Breukel on Tuesday morning; her farewells said, Sarah was driven away to the hospital and found the ambulance already there. Her stepfather was already in it; she could hear his irate voice complaining bitterly about something—a useless exercise as everyone there was occupied with getting Mrs Holt into the ambulance in her turn. Now that she was actually leaving she had become a bundle of doubts, and it was only when Sarah arrived that she would consent to get into the ambulance.

Sarah went round the small group of nurses and the two ward sisters, uttering thanks and offering the chocolates. They must be glad to see the back of us, she reflected, dragging out her goodbyes for as long as possible, just in case Mr ter Breukel should come.

There was no reason why he should; Suzanne had wished her goodbye on the previous evening, and they had parted with mutual regret that their friendship would have to end. She would have liked to have said goodbye to Mr ter Breukel, too, although she didn't think that *he* would feel any regret...

She couldn't spin the time out any longer, and went round to the front of the ambulance; she was to sit with the driver so that the paramedic with him could travel with her mother and stepfather. She reached up to open the door, and Mr ter Breukel's large hand lifted her hand away and opened it for her.

'Have a safe journey,' he told her. 'Make sure that you get all the documents before you board the plane, the driver will let you have them at Schiphol. I've written to your doctor, of course, and sent the X-rays to him; if he needs to know anything further he can reach me here.'

Sarah nodded. Now that she was actually seeing him for the last time she could think of nothing to say. If only she could think of something which would remind him of her—she frowned fiercely at the ridiculous idea and offered a hand. She said, 'Thank you for all that you have done. Everyone has been so kind and we must have been a nuisance…'

He didn't deny that, but said, 'You have been happy here, despite the circumstances?'

'Yes, oh, yes.'

He smiled then, still holding her hand, and then gave it back to her and opened the door. Sarah whispered, 'Goodbye,' and got in, because there was nothing else that she could do. She could have got out again, of course, and refused to go, causing confusion and embarrassment to everyone there. For one wild moment she considered this, but only for a moment. She smiled and waved and was driven away, back to Clapham.

The journey went smoothly, despite untold hold-ups and complaints from the Holts, and they arrived in the late afternoon to find Mrs Twist, the house-keeper, waiting for them.

This was by far the hardest part of the journey for Sarah. She had coped well enough with documents, passports, various officials, her mother's endless de-mands and her stepfather's rantings, but now, once more in their own house, they both demanded instant attention.

Her mother wished to be put to bed immediately, and cosseted with a light meal, the male nurse who had been engaged to attend to Mr Holt hadn't arrived, and although Mr Holt was quite able to do a good deal for himself he also demanded assistance, and Mrs Twist, good soul though she was, found it all a bit too much and retired to the kitchen in tears.

It was long past midnight by the time the house was at last quiet and Sarah could take herself off to bed. The nurse hadn't turned up. It was to be hoped that he would arrive in the morning…

Dr Benson came first. Mrs Twist and Sarah had just finished dealing with breakfast, and Sarah, who had known him for some years, welcomed him with open arms, handed over the various letters and papers she had been given and then went to admit the nurse. He was a sober, middle-aged man, who looked capable of dealing with her stepfather's ill temper. He would come each day, he told her, for a couple of hours in the morning and again in the early evening.

Which left a good deal of the day during which Mr Holt would expect attention. But now that her mother was well again she could perhaps be persuaded to spend an hour or two with him each afternoon, thought Sarah hopefully.

They settled down to an uneasy routine, for Mrs Holt couldn't be relied upon to keep to any routine, and was liable to go off for an afternoon's shopping in a taxi without warning anyone, returning exhausted and demanding Sarah's instant attention.

It was on Dr Benson's third visit that he brought his partner with him: Robert Swift, a young man with a cheerful face and a friendly way with him.

Over a cup of coffee, after visiting his patient, he

told Sarah that he intended to stay in Clapham. 'I've got rooms here,' he told her, 'but I'm getting married next year and we've got our eyes on a rather nice flat close to the Common. We're both Londoners and Jennie likes it here. I'm jolly lucky to be taken on as Dr Benson's partner.'

Sarah liked him and listened, whenever he called, to his hopes for the future while he drank the coffee she always had ready for him.

They had been back a week when he suggested that she might like to go with him to see the flat he hoped to buy. 'I told Jennie about you,' he told her ingenuously. 'She's gone up to Yorkshire to nurse an aunt. You've lived here for a few years, haven't you, so you would know if it's in a decent part of Clapham. We want somewhere nice; I don't want Jennie to work when we're married.'

'I'd love to come. It would have to be when Kenneth's here—but the morning's no good for you, is it? He comes back each afternoon about five o'clock and stays for two hours.'

'Suits me! How about tomorrow? It's my half-day.' He gave her a friendly look. 'You don't get much time to yourself, do you?'

'Not just at the moment, but my stepfather is to have crutches very soon, and that will be a lot easier.'

A statement not to be believed for one moment. Mr Holt on crutches would be a menace, going round the house, interfering with all and sundry. Now, more or less chained to his bed, he had to be content to supervise his business by telephone, and an occasional visit from one of his underlings, but once up and

about there would be no holding him. He wouldn't
be able to drive the new car which had replaced the
damaged one, which meant that Sarah would be expected to chauffeur him if he took a fancy to go to
the office. And that would annoy her mother, who
regarded her as an unpaid companion.

She must escape, but how?

Robert Swift arrived punctually the next day, and
since Kenneth was already in the house Sarah went
away to put on her outdoor things, find her mother
and explain that she would be back within the hour.
Robert was waiting in the hall and they went to the
door together. It was a rather hideous door, with coloured glass panels and a loud bell. Somebody was
ringing it now; she opened the door, laughing at
something Robert had said as she did so.

Mr ter Breukel stood there.

'Oh, it's you,' cried Sarah. 'Oh, I never expected…!' Delight at the sight of him had taken her
breath.

Mr ter Breukel said, in a calm voice which allowed
none of his feelings to show, 'Hello, Sarah. I'm over
here for a short while and thought I would look you
up, but I see I've called at an awkward time. Don't
let me keep you.'

'You're not—that is, we're only going to look at a
flat. This is Dr Swift.' She looked at Robert. 'Mr ter
Breukel is a consultant surgeon at the hospital where
my stepfather and mother were…'

Mr ter Breukel offered a hand. 'They're doing well,
I hope?'

'Yes—I'm only Dr Benson's junior partner, sir. Did you wish to see them? I'm sure Dr Benson…'

'No, no. I'll be phoning him before I go back to Holland. I'm sure they are in excellent hands.'

He smiled down at Sarah. 'I'm glad to see you looking so well and happy, Sarah. Suzanne sent her love.'

'She did? You'll come and see us before you go?'

He said smoothly, 'I doubt if I'll have the time. And I mustn't keep you from viewing this flat.' He looked at Robert. 'You intend to settle here?'

'Oh, yes. We both know this part of London well, and it's a splendid practice.'

Mr ter Breukel offered a hand again. 'Then I must wish you a happy future. And you too, of course, Sarah.' He smiled. 'It didn't take you long to discover that Clapham has its advantages over Arnhem.'

His handshake was brief, and she was still gathering her woolly wits together when he turned, walked down the short drive, got into his car and drove away.

'He seems a nice chap,' said Robert. 'Not so young, of course. But good at his job, I dare say.'

Sarah swallowed the tears which had kept her silent. 'He's very nice, and he's quite young and very clever. Shall we go? I mustn't be away for too long.'

Robert was too full of his own plans to notice her silence. She admired the flat, agreed that it was in a good neighbourhood and would make a perfect home for his Jennie, and presently he drove her back.

'I won't ask you in,' she told him at the door. 'Mother expects me to see to her supper and help get her ready for bed.'

'Of course. But surely Mrs Holt feels quite fit again?'

'Well, yes, Dr Benson says she's very well, but she—she suffers from her nerves and likes someone to—to be with her…'

Robert gave her a thoughtful look. 'A companion sounds the right answer to that. Wouldn't you like to be independent—find a job?'

'Very much, but it's not very easy at the moment. Perhaps when my stepfather is quite recovered.' She added, in a bitter little voice, 'But, you see, I'm not trained for anything.'

'There are dozens of things you could do—a few months' training at whatever you choose and you're on your way.'

'You're right, Robert, and I'll see what I can do about it. You must think me a very spineless person.'

'No, you're a dutiful daughter tied by the leg.' He grinned suddenly. 'You have nice legs too. Goodbye, Sarah, I'll be in some time tomorrow.'

Sarah managed not to think too much about Mr ter Breukel that evening, but later, in bed, lying awake thinking about him, going over their brief meeting word for word, was quite suddenly struck by an appalling thought, He had asked about Robert's flat, but Robert hadn't mentioned his Jennie, and then Mr ter Breukel had wished them both a happy future, and that would explain his remark about her liking Clapham better than Arnhem.

He thought that she and Robert were going to marry. What must he think of her after she had told him so plainly that she had no plans to marry, no boyfriend, and had let him see that she liked him?

And she had no idea where he was; she couldn't write and explain, let alone go and see him. He was in London, she supposed, but London was vast… She told herself to be sensible, and to think sensibly too. Presently she got out of bed and searched through her handbag. Sure enough, Suzanne had written down her phone number. 'So that we can give each other a ring from time to time,' she had said. And I will, decided Sarah, as soon as possible in the morning.

She got back into bed, and presently cried herself to sleep.

Breakfast dealt with, she went to her stepfather's study and dialled Suzanne's number. 'It's me,' she said in answer to a sleepy hello. 'Sarah. Mr ter…that is, your brother came to see us yesterday, only I was just going out and I—I wanted to see him but he went away and I don't know where he is. If I did I could go and see him or phone him…'

She wasn't being very sensible; Suzanne must think she was being silly.

Suzanne, who had known that Litrik was going to England, added two and two together and made five before Sarah could speak again.

'He's in London for several days. I'll give you his number and his address, and he'll be at two or three hospitals. Wait while I get my pocketbook.'

She read out the numbers, added addresses and advised Sarah to go and see him. 'You know how it is if you phone. Some dragon tells you he isn't there or he's engaged with a patient. That first address I gave you is the most likely—he'll be seeing private patients there in the mornings between nine o'clock and noon while he's in London. Nice to hear from you, Sarah.'

Her mother didn't take kindly to the idea of Sarah going off at a moment's notice that morning, but Sarah went all the same. She hadn't enough money for a taxi, and anyway her mother would want to know exactly why she needed to go somewhere in such a hurry, but the rush hour was over and a bus shouldn't take too long. However, she had reckoned without an unkind Fate; an accident held up the traffic, buses were diverted... She reached the hospital at five minutes to twelve, and by the time she had asked her way to the wing used for consulting rooms it was five past the hour. And Mr ter Breukel, she was told, had been gone for five minutes.

'You don't know where?' asked Sarah of the receptionist.

The girl unwrapped a chocolate bar and took a bite. 'No idea. He won't be here in the hospital again today. You're not a patient?'

Sarah shook her head. 'No—I—it doesn't matter.'

So she went back home and, being a girl who liked to finish what she had started, studied the phone numbers and addresses Suzanne had given her. She decided against ringing him up—either one talked too much or too little on the phone—but there was a likely address. She looked it up on the street map in her stepfather's study and decided that it must be a private house, close to Harley Street. Either he would have rooms there or it was a service flat. If he was working he would hardly be at a hotel.

Her mind made up, she helped Mrs Twist with lunch, spent the afternoon with her mother, had tea with her and took tea to her stepfather, then went to the kitchen to help Mrs Twist with dinner.

The evening would be the best time to go and see Mr ter Breukel, she had decided, and to strike while the iron was hot seemed good sense. Kenneth had arrived, and would be with her stepfather for a couple of hours, and friends had called to see her mother.

'I'm going out,' she told Mrs Twist. 'I don't expect I'll be very long. I'll tell Mother before I go, but don't fuss if I'm not back in time for dinner.'

It was a chilly evening, but light, so she put on a coat over her jersey dress, did her face and hair carefully, told her mother that she would be back presently and set out once more. It was quite a long journey and she had ample time to rehearse what she wanted to say. She wouldn't stay, of course—after a day's work he would be tired—but she had to explain...

The address she had been given was one of a row of rather grand houses with steps leading up to their important front doors. Not the kind of house one would have expected to have been turned into flats. The curtains were drawn across the windows but there was a light showing through the transom above the door. She glanced at her watch; it was almost eight o'clock—later than she had thought, but it was too late to turn back now. She thumped the great brass knocker.

The door was opened by a severe-looking maid, very correctly dressed in a black dress with a white apron.

'Mr ter Breukel?' asked Sarah. 'He is staying here, I believe?'

'Yes, miss.' The girl wasn't unfriendly and Sarah took heart.

'Could I see him for a few minutes? If you would take my name…'

The girl stood aside and Sarah passed her into an elegant hall. 'Who shall I say, miss?'

'Sarah Beckwith—Miss.' She followed the girl across the hall and was close behind her when she opened one of the doors. The room, large, splendidly furnished and brilliantly lighted, was full of people dressed for the evening, drinks in their hands, and right at the end of it she could see Mr ter Breukel, elegant in black tie, talking to a group of equally elegant men and women.

The maid had left her, and Sarah, good sense flown out of her head, stood where she was, rooted to the spot. This was something she hadn't even imagined. She saw the maid speak to Mr ter Breukel and he looked up and saw her. He was a good way off, but near enough for her to see that he wasn't smiling. A belated idea to get out of the house as quickly as possible was nipped in the bud, because now he had spoken to a man nearby and was crossing the room.

'Oh, dear,' said Sarah and backed away. She would apologise for disturbing his evening and leave smartly…

His 'Good evening, Sarah,' was uttered in a voice

which told her nothing, and after she asked the maid where they might go she followed him meekly across the hall and into a small room, cosily furnished and rather untidy. There was a large ginger cat curled up before the small fire, who took no notice of them as they went in.

'Do sit down,' said Mr ter Breukel. 'You wanted to see me urgently? Your parents?'

Sarah sat down on a small easy chair and the cat jumped onto her lap and was instantly asleep. She took one or two deep breaths, because she had read somewhere that that was the way to calm one's nerves.

'I'm sorry, I didn't know that you would be having a party. I tried to see you at the hospital this morning, but you had gone. There was a hold-up and the bus had to make a detour—the passengers got very annoyed, but really it wasn't the driver's fault...' She stopped, aware that she wasn't getting to the point, and Mr ter Breukel, watching her, fell in love with her all over again.

He said gently, 'You wanted to see me?'

She gave him a grateful glance. 'Yes, about yesterday. If I'd have known that you would be coming to see us, I would have told Robert not to come.'

'A wise decision...'

'Yes, well, you see, I could go and see the flat at any time—that is, when he's free—but you were unexpected, and anyway I didn't think fast enough. I should have told Robert to go away.'

'He seems a very pleasant young man. Only a little older than yourself?'

'He's thirty. I'm twenty-three. But you know that. What I wanted to make quite clear....' Her thoughts, darting here and there like mice in a trap, had taken on a life of their own. 'Do you live here? Suzanne gave me this address. It's a very nice house.'

Mr ter Breukel said with careful nonchalance, 'She phones you from time to time, I expect? She likes you.'

'I like her, too; she's so pretty. No, I phoned her. You see, I wanted to see you and make things clear.'

He crossed one leg over the other. Presumably his Sarah would soon come to the point. She was behaving as though she felt guilty about this Robert. He felt a dull despair at the thought of her marrying him, but if she was going to be happy then he would learn to live without her. He had allowed himself to daydream; he should have known better at his age. What girl would want to marry a man twelve years older than she?

Somewhere in the house a gong sounded, and Sarah said, 'Oh, dear, that's for dinner. You must go.'

'We haven't got very far, have we?' he said, and his voice was kind. 'You have been trying to tell me that you're going to marry Robert and for some reason you're scared to do so. I'm delighted for you, Sarah, and I'm sure you will be very happy.'

The door opened behind them and a young woman poked her head round it.

'Forgive me, but we're just going in to dinner. Perhaps your friend would like to stay?'

Sarah had got to her feet. 'No, no. I was just going. I'm sorry to have interrupted.'

She smiled at the young woman, who smiled back and disappeared down the hall. 'Come when you are ready, Litrik,' she called over a shoulder.

The maid was in the hall, waiting to open the door. Sarah made for it in a rush. To get out of the house and away from Mr ter Breukel was vital, for once out in the street she could cry as much as she wanted. She had made a fine mess of everything, but perhaps that was a good thing for he had said that he was delighted that she would be marrying Robert.

She put out a hand and had it shaken gently, muttered something, she had no idea what, and left the house very nearly at a run. If he had said anything to her she hadn't heard him, but really there was nothing more to say, was there? She began to walk very fast, letting the buses pass her. She had been a fool; all her carefully rehearsed speeches had been forgotten and she had talked a lot of rubbish—and anyway, what did it matter to him if she married someone else? Why had she been so anxious to explain his mistake in thinking that?

She gave a great gulping sob. She wasn't going to get married anyway. 'And I dare say I never shall,' she said, and a passer-by gave her a wary look.

She caught a bus presently, and went home to face Mrs Twist's anxious face, her mother's complaining voice and her stepfather roaring from his room.

'Not one of my best days,' said Sarah to herself later, gobbling her warmed-up dinner at the kitchen table. Mrs Twist had gone to bed, and presently she would set about settling her stepfather and her mother for the night.

She went to bed after that and, contrary to her expectations, slept at once. But she woke in the early hours, her mind very clear.

'It's funny I didn't think of it sooner. Of course I wanted to explain to him—because I'm in love with him.'

She felt a warm glow of happiness at the thought, but in the pale early-morning light common sense took over; the glow was still there but she must learn to keep it tucked away, out of sight and mind.

CHAPTER FOUR

FOR the next few days the hope that she would see Mr ter Breukel again coloured Sarah's dull daily round. She didn't sleep well, but each morning she got out of bed telling herself that surely he would phone her, or even come to say goodbye before he went back to Holland. And each night she went to bed and wept quietly. Not because she had hoped that they would meet again, but because he had seemed so pleased that she was, as he'd presumed, to marry Robert.

He would think nothing of her for keeping Robert up her sleeve, as it were, while accepting his friendship. And that was all it was, she reminded herself; she didn't expect anything warmer than that, but to have him as a friend would have been a wonderful thing.

Loving someone who didn't love you, reflected Sarah one night, mopping her eyes and blowing her small red nose, was very painful. She gave a great sniff and curled up in bed, wondering where he was and what he was doing. It was comforting, somehow, to know that somewhere out there, in the world she had so little chance of seeing much of, he would be working and eating and sleeping just as she was.

Which was exactly what he was doing. But, unlike her, he viewed the future in a different light. If Sarah was happy, if she wanted to marry this young doctor, then he would accept that, but first he had to be quite sure that this was so, and he *wasn't* sure…

Unlike Sarah, his days were full; he thrust her image to the back of his mind and dealt with consultations, clinics, patients and sessions in the operating theatre, as at home in the London hospitals as he was at Arnhem. He had been a consultant at both hospitals for some years now, and came to London several times a year. Nevertheless he did have opportunities to drive to Clapham Common and see Sarah, all of which he ignored.

If she were going to marry Robert then she would have little interest in another visit from him, and the thin thread of their friendship might snap. And he must still find out more about her and Robert; only when he knew with certainty that they were to marry would he abandon his hopes for the future.

Two weeks later, on the point of his return to Arnhem, he telephoned Dr Benson, enquired as to Mr Holt's progress and, after a brief discussion, observed with just the right amount of interest that he had met the doctor's young partner.

Dr Benson was enthusiastic about him. 'A good doctor, and already well liked by my patients. He's getting married shortly—his future wife, Jennie, is a very nice girl, familiar with this area, too. They're busy getting their flat ready. They intended to marry next year, but since they've found this place and he's settled in so well there's no reason for them not to set up home sooner. Some time in May, I believe. If you're over here by any chance you must come to the wedding—and take a look at Mr Holt at the same time. I quite understand that your commitments prevented you from seeing him this time, but I can assure you that your good work will be continued here.'

'I feel sure of that. And Mrs Holt and her daughter?'

'Mrs Holt is quite herself again, a nervous and delicate lady, as you no doubt know, depending very much upon her daughter. And Sarah seems none the worse for the accident. She is rather a quiet girl, and seems even quieter now. She really needs to be independent and leave home, but of course she has no training, and Mrs Holt relies upon her for everything. She meets very few young people…'

All of which Mr ter Breukel thought about deeply as he took himself back to Arnhem. The overwhelming relief at discovering that it wasn't Sarah who was to marry Robert was overshadowed by concern for her happiness. His first impulse was to carry her off and marry her out of hand, but she might have other wishes as to her future. Probably she regarded him as a rather staid man to whom she owed gratitude.

She had told him something of her life, but very little about her own hopes for the future. For all he knew she might want to travel, become a career girl, go on the stage. He must, he told himself, on no account be impatient, and if possible think of some means whereby she might become independent and see something of the world, even if it were only another part of London. Only then would he find a way of resuming their friendship and finally marrying her.

He needed to think about it, but only after he had tackled the backlog of patients and operations waiting for him at St Bravo's.

That done, he set about his problem with calm logic. Suzanne first, for he wanted her opinion of the prospects of a job for a girl without any kind of training.

She said at once, 'Oh, you're thinking of Sarah. Why don't you marry her, Litrik? Then she won't need to get work.'

'That's an easy answer, my dear. But Sarah's never had a chance to spread her wings. Suppose she were to marry me and then discover that what she wanted was a career of some sort, a chance to meet people— men—of her own age? No, she must have a little time to discover what she really wants.'

Suzanne thought. 'Well, I'd look for a job where all that was needed was common sense and a willingness to do anything wanted.' She shrugged. 'Sounds hopeless, doesn't it?'

'No, it makes sense. It will have to be work where I can keep her under my eye.'

'What about the hospital—the London one?'

'I had thought of that, and that is a possibility, but I have to find a way to get her there...'

Suzanne gave him a sisterly peck on the cheek. 'And you will, Litrik. Let me know if I can help, won't you?'

Mr ter Breukel had many friends, some of them colleagues of long standing at the London hospital. He was on good terms with the hospital manager, too, and it was through him, by asking carefully casual questions, that he discovered that there was a shortage of unskilled labour in the kitchens, the house doctors' rooms and dining room, and in the staff canteen.

The kitchens wouldn't do at all, and nor would the house doctors' quarters; he wasn't so old that he couldn't remember that young housemen tended to relax like small boys when they had the chance... It would have to be the canteen.

Having settled that, his next problem was somewhat harder to solve. How to get her away from Clapham Common? He ignored her stepfather—the man was a bully, and lacking in any kind feeling towards her, but he wouldn't be able to stop Sarah leaving home. It was her mother who would do that if she could, playing upon Sarah's kind heart and her sense of duty. Mr ter Breukel sat at his desk night after night, with the faithful Max at his feet, and bent his powerful brain to the matter.

To good effect. The series of telephone calls he eventually made were entirely satisfactory, even though they were protracted and necessitated a good deal of discussion. The impossible, reflected Mr ter Breukel, is sometimes possible, provided one is determined enough. And he *was* determined.

Mr Holt's leg confining him to the house and depriving Mrs Holt of participating in their normal social life meant that she was unable to enjoy herself as she would wish. She had friends—but friends who were loath to invite her to dinner parties without her husband, unwilling for her to join in their usual social round on her own. She had to fall back on bridge afternoons and shopping and the occasional meeting for coffee while shopping. As a consequence her discontent grew, as did her peevishness, and since there was no one else she vented both on Sarah.

'It is a pity that you're not pretty and socially minded,' she complained, 'then at least there would be some young people about the house.'

To which Sarah said nothing, although she could have pointed out that young people had never been encouraged. She remembered with shame the few occasions when she had invited schoolfriends home and watched her mother with subtle charm eclipse her own efforts. Later on it had been worse, for such young men as she'd met had occasionally found her mother's pretty ways and gentle manner quite irresistible...

Now, as far as she could see, the faint hopes that she could persuade her mother to let her find work were fading. Sarah had brought the matter up already, on several occasions, and her mother had told her with a pitiful smile that she must please herself; no mother would prevent her child from doing what they wished, however selfish that child was.

The days seemed endless to Sarah, although she didn't allow her despondency to get the upper hand. She had plenty to do—shopping, helping with the ironing and cooking, giving Mrs Twist a hand around the house, paying dutiful visits to her stepfather, listening to her mother's complaining voice. Days in which she had very little time to herself.

And a good thing too, she told herself; if she had time on her hands she would waste it thinking about

Mr ter Breukel, who, she assured herself a dozen times a day, meant nothing to her. She would, in time, be able to discard her love for him. She reflected that it was probably a flash in the pan, engendered by her lack of men-friends. Probably she would have fallen in love with the first man she met, given the circumstances…

It was April now, quite warm and sunny. Sarah was in the garden, casting an eye over the tubs she had planted in the autumn, when Mrs Twist called her indoors.

'Yer ma wants yer, Miss Sarah. Very excited about something.'

Mrs Holt was in her bedroom, sitting at the dressing table, making up her pretty face. 'Sarah—get my new grey dress for me. I've had a phone call from Dr Benson. He's bringing some important specialist to see your stepfather. For heaven's sake, tidy yourself, and then go and get coffee ready. They'll be here in half an hour.'

'Didn't you say they're coming to see my stepfather?'

'Yes. But they'll want to know how *I* am. I'm sure I'll never be the same again after that horrible accident.' She glanced at Sarah. 'Get the coffee ready first, Sarah, then do something to your hair. *You* won't need to see them, of course, but I suppose you'll bring in the coffee.'

Sarah paused at the door. 'Mother, if you don't want me to be seen, you could fetch the coffee from the kitchen yourself.'

'Sarah, what a dreadful way to speak to your

mother. You know how delicate my nerves are.' Mrs
Holt touched a handkerchief to a dry eye. 'Now I'm
upset.'

Sarah went away and got the tray ready, with the
best china and a little dish of assorted biscuits. She
popped two into her mouth and crossed the hall to
the cloakroom. The breeze in the garden had ruffled
her tidy hair, and she supposed that she had better run
a comb through it. She was halfway across the hall
when the doorbell was rung. She glanced at the long
case clock by the stairs; it was far too soon for Dr
Benson and this specialist—the postman, maybe, or
someone trying to make a living selling dusters at the
door? She opened the door and came face to face with
Dr Benson.

'Oh, hello,' said Sarah. 'You're early. Mother said
half an hour.' She smiled at him, for they were old
friends, and then looked past him to the youngish man
standing quietly behind him.

'This is Professor Smythe. I thought it a good idea
if he were to cast an eye over your stepfather. And
perhaps your mother would be glad of a word?'

Sarah held out a hand. 'I'm sure Mother and my
stepfather will be glad to see you. Do come in.' She
led the way to the drawing room. 'I'll fetch Mother.
Would you like a cup of coffee?'

'Perhaps after we have seen Mr Holt?' Dr Benson
looked at the professor, who nodded. 'Ah, here is
your mother.'

Mrs Holt's voice could be heard through the half-
open door, wanting to know who had rung the door-
bell and why hadn't Sarah told her? She sounded

cross, but as she came into the room and saw the two men she smiled charmingly. 'Dr Benson, how kind of you to come...' She turned to the professor and smiled even more charmingly. 'And this is the consultant you mentioned?'

'Professor Smythe, Mrs Holt. He will examine Mr Holt and give me any necessary advice.'

'I have been so anxious about him,' said Mrs Holt, offering a hand. 'I'm sure you're terribly clever. It was such a shock—the accident, you know. I feel that I shall never completely recover.'

The professor murmured. He would have a lovely bedside manner, thought Sarah, watching him from the door and then watching the three of them go upstairs to her stepfather's room. She didn't know if her mother had told Mr Holt of the impending visit, but whether he knew or not he would be annoyed by it.

They were upstairs for a long time. Sarah, keeping the coffee hot in the kitchen, ate two more biscuits, and when they finally came downstairs, she carried the tray into the drawing room. The professor took it from her with a smile, and sat down opposite Mrs Holt, while Sarah passed round cups and the biscuits.

'Sarah, run along, dear. I'm sure you don't want to be bored with our talk. Besides, I want a little chat with these two kind men. I've made light of my troubles, but I do feel that I need professional help.'

Sarah didn't say anything, but the professor put his cup and saucer down and went to open the door for her. She looked at him as she went past. He had a kind face and was smiling.

She shared a pot of tea with Mrs Twist and, since

she had nothing else to do, sat at the kitchen table chopping up vegetables for the casserole which Mrs Twist was intending to cook.

They were a long time, she thought uneasily, then looked up as the door opened and Professor Smythe came in.

Sarah jumped up. 'Have you lost your way? The drawing room's on the other side of the house—down the passage and across the hall.'

'No. No, I wish to talk to you.' He glanced at Mrs Twist and smiled, and that lady put down the knife with which she had been cutting up the meat.

'You'd best stay here,' she said. 'I've plenty to get on with upstairs.'

He opened the door for her and thanked her with another smile, and then pulled out a chair and sat down opposite Sarah.

'You really shouldn't be here in the kitchen,' said Sarah. 'I mean, you're a professor...'

'I like kitchens.' He had a pleasant voice, very quiet. 'We always have breakfast in our kitchen; it's so much easier with two small children.'

'Boys or girls?'

'One of each, soon to be joined by a third.'

'How nice... I mustn't waste your time. Did you want to tell me something? Is Mother ill?' she asked worriedly.

'Your mother is in the best of health, but I have suggested certain changes which might improve her physically and mentally.'

When Sarah gave him a questioning look he said, 'Your mother is bored; she needs a complete change in her lifestyle. Dr Benson and I have had a chat and he fully endorses my suggestion that your mother and stepfather should close the house for a period and spend time at a hotel, somewhere where your mother can enjoy something of a social life. Your stepfather can be given all the attention he wants—massage, daily visits from a nurse—for a gradual return to the full use of his leg. I suggested Bournemouth—good hotels, shops, entertainment, access to private nursing facilities. I understand that there will be no financial problems…'

Sarah opened her mouth, closed it, and shook her head. She didn't speak but her eyes looked a question.

'Your mother agrees with me that a fresh environment and new faces would be ideal, and I suggested that she would benefit greatly from meeting people about whom she knew nothing and who knew nothing of her and your stepfather. I think that it would be wise if you do not go with them, and your mother has been persuaded that this is the right thing to do.'

'I don't have to go, too? I can stay here with Mrs Twist?' Sarah beamed at him. 'For how long? You're sure Mother won't change her mind and I'd have to go, too?'

'Quite sure, and we've suggested a period of two to three months.'

He watched her face light up. A plain girl, but nice eyes, and when she smiled she looked almost beautiful. No wonder Litrik was interested in her. The things one does for one's old friends, reflected Professor Smythe.

'Dr Benson has made a most sensible suggestion,'

he went on smoothly. 'Why not get a job while you are here with the housekeeper? It will fill your days, and you will meet people and earn some money.'

'I'd like that very much, but you see I'm not trained for anything. When I left school Mother wasn't very well, and she gets very upset if I suggest leaving home.'

'Then why not take this opportunity to try your hand at something? There are jobs which require little or no training, you know. I'm sure Dr Benson can advise you.'

Sarah sat up straight in her chair. 'Oh, my goodness, wouldn't it be absolutely marvellous?' She sounded like a schoolgirl, he thought, and looked like one too in her skirt and sweater. He had noticed that Mrs Holt was dressed fashionably. Either her daughter had no dress sense, or no money with which to buy pretty clothes. He had formed a low opinion of her stepfather—not a man to open a generous purse.

'Then shall we go and tell your mother that you agree with us that a short period in new surroundings will be beneficial to her health?'

Sarah said yes; he sounded exactly as a professor should sound, very sure of himself.

Her mother was talking animatedly to Dr Benson, but broke off to exclaim, 'Sarah, is this not a splendid idea of these two kind gentlemen? And your stepfather has agreed. You won't blame your poor little mother for leaving you alone for a few weeks? You will have Mrs Twist. I know that we shall return completely cured and able to resume our normal lives again.'

Sarah eyed her mother with patient tolerance. 'It's a splendid idea, Mother. I shall be quite all right here with Mrs Twist.'

'That's what I thought, dear. There must be many things you want to do, and now you will have the time.'

Sarah agreed pleasantly, and tried not to look too pleased.

The two men left presently, and her mother went to discuss their plans with her husband. So Sarah went to the kitchen and gave Mrs Twist an account of the doctor's visit, leaving out the news that she intended to go to work. Mrs Twist was a dear soul, and her staunch friend, but there was just a chance that she might inadvertently let the cat out of the bag.

Now that the decision had been taken, Mrs Holt lost no time. Hotel brochures were scanned, dates were decided upon, and a good deal of shopping was done—for a new environment needed new clothes. It was left to Sarah to search out a nursing agency who would send a nurse and a masseuse each day to the hotel, and it was she who booked rooms at a splendid hotel on the seafront. When it came to his own comfort, her stepfather spent lavishly, and just as lavishly but rather less willingly on his wife.

He was less concerned for Sarah. He arranged for expenses for the household to be paid weekly, together with Mrs Twist's wages, and in a sudden display of generosity told Sarah that if she needed money for any other reason she could ask him for it.

'As long as it's a reasonable amount,' he cautioned

her. 'This is an expensive undertaking. If anyone at the office should need me urgently, refer them to me.'

Mr ter Breukel, kept up to date by his friend Professor Smythe, was satisfied. The next step would be taken by Dr Benson, primed by him after another satisfactory phone call to the hospital manager in London.

Mr ter Breukel possessed his soul in patience and waited for the next move in his scheme.

The removal to Bournemouth was almost as big an undertaking as the journey back from Holland had been. Mr Holt had a new car now, and a hired chauffeur, and between them he and Mrs Holt had a vast quantity of luggage. And the business of getting him comfortable with a leg still in a small plaster took time and the efforts of several persons. But at last he pronounced himself satisfied, Sarah's mother got in beside him, the chauffeur got behind the wheel and drove away. Sarah and Mrs Twist waved, but went unnoticed.

The pair of them went back to the kitchen, and over a pot of tea Sarah told her plans. 'Of course I have to find a job,' she explained, 'and that might take a few days. You won't mind? I'll find work where I can come home each evening. Oh, Mrs Twist, it's the chance I've always hoped for and never thought I'd get—not without running away in the middle of the night. But that wouldn't have been very practical…'

Mrs Twist pronounced the scheme a good one. 'High time a young lady like you got out and about a bit—never a moment to yourself. What'll yer do?'

'I've no idea…' But she was soon to find out.

It was two days later when Dr Benson called. Sarah was in the kitchen, working her way through the 'Jobs Vacant' columns of several newspapers. She had already searched the adverts in *The Lady* magazine, and marked several likely posts, but most of them were out of London. The local paper might be more fruitful. She looked up as Mrs Twist ushered the doctor into the kitchen and got to her feet.

'Dr Benson—is something wrong? Mother? My stepfather?'

'No, no, Sarah, my visit concerns yourself. You do remember we talked about you finding a job?' His eye fell on the pile of newspapers. 'You're looking for something? Well, unless you've arranged anything, I've heard of something you might care to try. Perhaps not quite your touch, but it would give you a start if you really want to strike out on your own.'

'Oh, I do. I'll do anything—well, not computers or typing or anything clever, and I don't think I'd be much good in a shop…'

'No skill needed for this job. Just patience and a friendly manner and an ability to stay on your feet for hours.' At her questioning look he added, 'The canteen at one of the hospitals is desperately short of staff. Serving meals, clearing away, fetching and carrying. Long hours, and shift work—twelve o'clock until eight in the evening, five days a week—but you wouldn't have to work on Saturday or Sunday. It's not much, I know, but you would meet people, Sarah, and it seems to me that that is something you have never had the chance of doing, other than your mother's bridge partners and your stepfather's business acquaintances.' He added, 'The pay's not much…'

When he told her she said, 'Not much? And I can spend it on myself, clothes and things?'

'Of course. Look, I'll give you the phone number and you can ask for an interview. Here's the number. Use my name as a reference and don't go looking too smart.'

Sarah said matter-of-factly, 'I haven't any smart clothes. And thank you very much; I shall phone this morning.' She laughed suddenly. 'It's the first step towards my marvellous future.'

Dr Benson agreed. He hoped that Mr ter Breukel's schemes wouldn't go awry. He was pushing his luck, giving her the opportunity to savour an independent life. Would it not have been better to have snapped her up at once and carried her off to Holland? On second thoughts, Dr Benson felt not. Sarah, for all her unassuming ways, had always refused to be led, and her stepfather's dislike of her hadn't helped.

Sarah believed in striking while the iron was hot; she phoned the moment Dr Benson had left the house, and was given an appointment for the next morning.

It wasn't until she had entered the rather gloomy portals of the hospital that doubts assailed her. She was to be interviewed by someone called the Domestic Supervisor. She might be disliked on sight; her references might not be sufficient to please this personage. By the time Sarah had reached the door to which she had been directed, the Domestic Supervisor had become the female equivalent of an ogre!

The voice which bade her enter was small and high-pitched, and to her relief Sarah saw that her imagined ogre was a very small, very round woman, with salt and pepper hair screwed into a bun and a nice smile.

'Come in, dearie. Miss Beckwith, isn't it? Sit down while we have a little chat.'

Fifteen minutes later Sarah rose from the chair. The job was hers. She was to start on the following day at noon.

'You may find it a bit of a rush for a day or two, but the girls will help you. You'll get your dinner at two o'clock, tea at five. The canteen closes down then, until first suppers at seven o'clock, but you'll be kept busy getting them ready. Second supper is at eight o'clock, and that's when the night shift take over. Hard work, my dear, but we'll see how you get on, shall we? A week's notice on either side.'

Sarah went back to Clapham Common and told Mrs Twist all about it. They arranged their days to suit them both. 'And if by any chance my mother should ring up, would you just tell her I'm out? But I don't expect her to telephone during the day.'

'Wear comfortable shoes,' advised Mrs Twist. 'Your feet are going to kill you.'

They didn't kill her, but by the end of her shift they ached so much she thought that she would never be able to go to work the next morning. But that was in a weak moment; lying in a hot bath, after supper with Mrs Twist, she knew that of course she would go to work in the morning. What was more, she would continue to do so until she found better work.

She had enjoyed her day, she reflected, adding more hot water. Dressed in a striped cotton dress, a white pinny and a white cap, she had presented herself to the Head Counter Assistant, admitted cheerfully that she had very little idea as to what she had to do, and had been borne away by two middle-aged women who'd called her 'ducks', showed her where everything was and, when the food arrived, stood her in front of a great container of chips. 'Dole 'em out, and no need to be mean about it. A couple of spoons and a bit over. Give us a shout if yer in a fix.'

She had managed very well; it seemed that everyone ate chips, and some of the housemen on duty, unable to get to their own dining room, had had two helpings. And everyone had been so friendly, asking her name, making little jokes. Though it had shaken her a bit when she had been dishing out chips to a bunch of nurses, standing there with their plates and discussing an accident case which had been admitted that morning. Sarah had tried not to hear the details. Nurses, she'd thought, must be wonderful people— able to take the sight of broken bones and blood everywhere, and still pile their plates with a wholesome dinner....

The only part of her day which she hadn't enjoyed was coming home. It was quite a long journey to and from the hospital, and although the April evenings were light, by the time she'd got off the bus evening had closed in, and the five-minute walk to her home was through more or less deserted streets. But that was something to which she would become accustomed; she had never had the chance to be out on her own in the evenings, only in her mother's company, or going with her and her stepfather to some function when he considered it good for his public image to be seen as a kindly stepfather and devoted husband.

By the end of the week her feet had accustomed themselves to standing for long periods, she had learnt her way around the canteen, made friends with the other girls and was on nodding terms with the hungry hordes who came to eat. They were always in a hurry, either on duty, or off duty and hurrying to get away. She exchanged rather guarded chat with anyone who lingered to talk for a moment, and took care to note which of the ward sisters liked a salad instead of vegetables.

She was always famished by two o'clock, but none of them wasted much time over their meal; there was tea to get ready, the first of the staff would start trickling in at about half past three, and after a brief pause there would be a second round of tea…and then a rush to get suppers on the counter.

But she had enjoyed it. She had met more people in a week than she had in all the years since she left school, and she had a pay packet in her pocket. What mattered most was that she had been so busy that she had been able to banish Mr ter Breukel from her thoughts for minutes at a time…

She took Mrs Twist out to supper on Saturday evening, to a small restaurant in the High Street, and Mrs Twist, in a hat suitable to the occasion, ate her way through the three-course meal and pronounced it as well cooked as she herself could have done. 'A real treat,' she declared, 'eating something I haven't 'ad to cook meself.'

On Sunday Mrs Twist went to spend the day with her sister; Sarah washed her hair and her smalls, did her nails, read the Sunday papers from end to end and thought about Mr ter Breukel. Mrs Twist safely back, they had their supper and went to bed.

'I shall never see him again,' said Sarah, looking at the moon through a sudden rush of tears. She wiped them away at once, told herself not to be a sentimental fool and got into bed.

It was halfway through her second week, as she was on the point of going down to the basement to start another day's work, that the lift door beside the staircase opened and Mr ter Breukel got out.

He had seen her, of course. 'Ah, Sarah, how nice to see you again.'

Her heart was beating so loudly he must surely be able to hear it. She had gone very red, and then pale, and hadn't said a word.

She found her breath. 'I shall be late,' she told him, and flew down the stairs.

He stood watching her race away, smiling to himself. She reminded him of the White Rabbit in *Alice in Wonderland*. He glanced at his watch; she would be off duty at eight o'clock. He had a clinic that afternoon, and post-operative patients to see later, but he would be free by then.

Everyone in the canteen acknowledged that Sarah was a good worker, willing to help out and not afraid of hard work, but today she surpassed herself: she served the meals, cleaned the tables and laid them again, swabbed the floor where someone had upset a bottle of tomato sauce, even offered to stay on for an extra hour or two as they were short-handed that day. An offer which wasn't accepted.

'You've worked yourself to death,' it was pointed out to her. 'You'll go off at eight sharp and no nonsense.'

All the same she was held up at the last minute by one of the staff coming in for sandwiches for the operating theatre staff, so that when she got to the changing room everyone else had gone.

She'd had some half-formed idea that if she went out of the hospital in a bunch with the other girls and saw Mr ter Breukel there would be no need to speak to him. Indeed, she could pretend not to see him… Now she would have to hope that he would be gone or, better still, in Theatre, operating.

She changed rapidly and climbed the stairs to the ground floor, taking the last few steps with all the wariness of a rabbit coming out of its burrow. The corridor was empty; she skimmed down it and saw that there was no one in the entrance hall. It was a relief not to meet him, although she ached with disappointment. Just that one glimpse of him coming out of the lift had been enough to undo all her sternly suppressed feelings since she had last seen him.

She called goodnight to the porter and pushed open the heavy doors. April had turned contrary; it was cold and windy and heavy clouds threatened rain. She paused to button her coat collar, and found herself face to face with Mr ter Breukel.

For the second time that day she lost her tongue,

staring up at his face, trying to think of something suitable to say. Hello was a bit too familiar; good evening sounded all wrong. 'It's not a very nice evening,' said Sarah.

'Very unpleasant,' he agreed cheerfully. 'Shall we have a meal out, or go to your place?'

'But they're not there—Mother and my stepfather. They're in Bournemouth recuperating.'

'Indeed? Then let us find a restaurant.'

'No, no, I can't. I mean, it's very kind of you to ask me, but Mrs Twist's waiting for me with supper. She'll wonder where I am.'

'Then let us go to Clapham Common and perhaps you will invite me to supper?'

Sarah, mindful of her manners, invited him, then added, 'Why are you here?'

He popped her into the car and got in beside her. 'I come here to work fairly frequently. You're working at the hospital?'

'Yes. Dr Benson and a Professor Smythe came to see my stepfather, and they thought it would do him and mother good to go away for a while. So they're in Bournemouth, and since I'm at home with Mrs Twist Dr Benson suggested that I got a job.' She added defiantly, 'I serve the meals at the canteen.'

'You enjoy that? Meeting new faces, making friends? You must have missed that, Sarah?'

'Yes. When Mother and my stepfather come back I shall move out—find a room, get a better job if I can, train for something.'

She glanced at his hands on the wheel and looked

away quickly. They were large, beautifully kept, and they reminded her how very much she loved him.

He parked the car outside the house and went in with her. Mrs Twist, coming into the hall, gave him a shrewd look as Sarah introduced them.

'Pleased ter meet yer, I'm sure,' she told him, and took the hand that he held out. 'Staying for supper? It's steak and kidney pie and apple turnovers. Miss Sarah, you go into the drawing room and have a drink while I lay the table.'

Sarah frowned. 'Mrs Twist—it's all ready in the kitchen, isn't it?'

'I like kitchens,' said Mr ter Breukel, and smiled at Mrs Twist.

'Well, then, if you say so, sir.'

'I'll get the sherry,' said Sarah, and went to the drawing room.

Mr ter Breukel followed her, took the bottle from her, dropped a kiss on her cheek and said quietly, 'We must find time to talk, but not just yet.'

He smiled down at her. 'The pie smells delicious. Come and tell me about your job while we eat.'

CHAPTER FIVE

MRS TWIST was at first reluctant to eat her supper with Sarah and Mr ter Breukel. 'I know me place,' she had said sharply, but then under his kindly eye she had changed her mind.

'Well, if that's what you want, sir. I should've thought you'd want ter be on yer own, like, with Miss Sarah.'

'Ah, but you see Sarah and I have all the time in the world to be together.'

A remark which caused Sarah to give him a surprised look, which he met with a bland smile. He was putting Mrs Twist at her ease, she reflected.

The meal was a success; Mrs Twist was a great talker, and Mr ter Breukel was adept at maintaining a conversation, and if Sarah was rather silent no one noticed. They didn't hurry over it, and when it was eaten Mr ter Breukel accepted Mrs Twist's offer of a cup of tea with every appearance of pleasure, drinking the powerful brew with evident appreciation before helping to clear the table and then making his departure, saying all the right things to Mrs Twist, bidding Sarah a friendly goodnight, and driving away without fuss.

While Mrs Twist washed up Sarah set the table for breakfast.

'Now there's a man for you,' said Mrs Twist. 'A

real gent, even if 'e is a bit of a la-di-da. Fancy me eating me supper with the likes of 'im. Whatever would your ma say?'

'Well, she won't know,' said Sarah. 'I shan't tell, and you won't either.'

'Lor' bless you, no. Known 'im long?'

'Well, I don't really know him very well. He looked after my stepfather at the Arnhem hospital; he's a Consultant there too, as well as over here.'

'A bit lonely over here on his own?' Mrs Twist was dying of curiosity.

'I don't suppose so. He's well known at the hospital, I think, and he must have lots of friends.'

'Well, I dare say you'll see a bit more of 'im while 'e's 'ere.'

'I doubt it,' said Sarah. 'The senior staff don't come to the canteen.'

But they were in the same building, she reflected, and if she took the long way round to the canteen she might see him.

During the next few days, though, there wasn't so much as a glimpse of him. You wouldn't think, thought Sarah, that such a large man could become so invisible. And he *was* in the hospital; dishing dinners to a group of staff nurses, she couldn't help but overhear their gossip. Mr ter Breukel, it seemed, had won the hearts of all the nurses who had had the good fortune to encounter him.

Sarah swallowed a sharp pang of jealousy and told herself not to be a fool. The sooner he went back to Holland the better, she decided. Life would never be the same again without him, but at least she could make a new life for herself now that she had work. She wasn't sure what would be the next step, but she was determined that it would be up, taking her away from Clapham Common. A month or two more working in the canteen, and then she would apply for the night shift; the pay was better. Several of the girls had rooms close to the hospital; she would do the same, save what money she could, and look for a better job.

She told herself that she was happy and content, that the future was exciting; she would become a successful career woman. She had no idea how this was to be achieved, but the thought of it made her days bearable as each successive one went by without a sight of Mr ter Breukel.

And when at last she saw him again it was disastrous. It was the end of her shift, and, last as usual, she climbed the stairs with one of the housemen who had been to the canteen to gobble a hasty supper. He was a nice lad, and lonely, and so was she. They dawdled up the staircase, making the most of a few moments of idle conversation, not really interested in each other, only glad to talk to someone.

They lingered on the top step, reluctant to go their separate ways, and Mr ter Breukel, intent on whisking Sarah out for a meal, came to an abrupt silent halt. Sarah was laughing and the young doctor laughed too, enjoying the small interlude, and instead of going straight to the wards he turned to walk to the entrance with her, still talking.

It was then that Sarah saw Mr ter Breukel, walking

towards them, and she paused in mid-sentence, smiling her delight at the sight of him.

A pity he didn't know that; he went past them with a brief, unsmiling nod and turned into the consultants' room, shutting the door firmly behind him.

Sarah parted with her companion in the entrance hall, hardly aware of how she had got there. Mr ter Breukel could have smiled, even wished her good evening. Perhaps he didn't care to be on speaking terms with a member of the domestic staff. She dismissed that thought as unworthy of him, left the hospital and walked to the bus stop.

There was no reason, she told herself, why he *should* speak to her. He was doubtless a busy man; moreover, he must have many friends in London. Taking her home the other evening had been an impulsive gesture which he clearly didn't intend to repeat.

Mr ter Breukel closed the door gently, quelling a desire to slam it or wrench it open again and pluck Sarah away from the cheerful young man with her. He would like to shake her until her teeth rattled. Better still, he would like to wrap his arms round her and kiss her.

He did none of these things, but went and sat down in one of the leather chairs arranged round the sombre room. He had no reason to be angry; he had planned this deliberately so that Sarah would have a chance to be independent and meet people. Well, his plan was working. It was early days, though, he reminded himself. He must have patience still, leave her free to choose her friends, plan her future. He was deeply in love with her, but he wanted her to be happy even at the cost of his own happiness.

So the best part of another week went by; he would be returning to Holland soon now…

As for Sarah, she felt herself to be a seasoned worker now, with little time to brood. Only at the weekends, alone in the house while Mrs Twist visited friends or family, did she admit to herself that life wasn't very satisfactory. It would be better, of course, once she could forget Mr ter Breukel…

One Friday evening, her pay packet in her pocket, she left the hospital rather later than usual. There had been no one in the cloakroom to tell her that there was a rowdy demonstration over something or other making its way towards the streets around the hospital, and the porter, deep in his evening paper, hadn't seen her slip out of the doors. The other canteen staff had left in a bunch, so he had warned them, thinking that they were all there. It was only as the doors swung back that he looked up and caught a glimpse of Sarah, hurrying away. Too late to go after her, he decided, and someone would have told her to avoid the main roads.

Mr ter Breukel, on the point of departure, having done a ward round and taken a look at his operation cases for that day, spoke to the ward sister, wishing her good evening and a pleasant weekend. She remarked, 'I expect you've heard that there's some kind of demonstration coming this way, sir? Most of it is peaceful enough, but there are the usual rowdies roaming around, making trouble. The staff going off duty have been warned to avoid them.'

Mr ter Breukel glanced at the clock. Ten minutes past eight. Sarah would have left or be on the point of leaving. He bade Sister a courteous goodnight and went down to the entrance hall.

The porter put his paper down and stood up. Mr ter Breukel had that effect upon people, although he was unconscious of it.

'The canteen staff?' he asked. 'Have they left?'

'Yes, a minute or two after eight o'clock. I passed on the warning that they should keep clear of any disturbances.'

'And no one has left since?'

'Well, now you mention it, sir, someone slipped out while I had my back turned. She was halfway across the forecourt before I heard the door close.'

'You have no idea who it was?'

'No, sorry, sir, only she wasn't very big and she had a red umbrella.' He added unnecessarily, 'It's raining, sir.'

Mr ter Breukel thanked him politely and went out into the drizzle, walking fast. He knew which bus stop Sarah used, and he had seen the red umbrella before. He searched the queue there. There was no sign of her; she was already on her way home, then. He turned away and saw a red umbrella a long way ahead of him, and at the same time several groups of noisy youths marching arm-in-arm on the pavement, pushing aside all the people.

He lengthened his stride, ignoring the catcalls,

pushing and shoving. The pavement was almost empty of other people, who were prudently taking cover in doorways and shops. Sarah was in plain sight, and why she was ignoring the fracas around her was something he couldn't understand—until he saw that she was with someone, another woman, and that they were both burdened with shopping bags.

There were some side roads lined by small brick houses, their doors opening onto the pavement. He saw Sarah turn into one such road and reached the corner of it only a few yards behind her. The road was empty save for three youths running from its other end, swooping down on her and her companion, yelling and shouting. The woman dropped her shopping bags and struggled to open the door of a house, but she dropped the key from a shaking hand as the three youths rushed at them.

Sarah furled her umbrella and poked the nearest boy in the ribs, then she thumped his companion and would have done the same for the third, but he caught it and tore it from her hand, waved it wildly and swung it down...

It didn't reach its mark; Mr ter Breukel swept Sarah aside with one arm, lifted the youth by his coat collar and set him down in a sprawling heap on the pavement, then sent the other two tumbling after him.

They stared up at him; he might look like a gentleman, but he was certainly a giant, and for all they knew a prizefighter in his best suit out for a stroll. They edged themselves backwards, scrambled to their feet and rushed away.

Mr ter Breukel hadn't said a word; he wasn't

breathing fast either. He stooped, picked up the key and handed it to the woman, and then, since she was still all of a tremble, took it from her, opened the door and stood aside for her to go in. He handed in her shopping bags too, assuring her that she was now quite safe, then brushed aside her thanks, waiting patiently while she thanked Sarah at some length and at last closed her door.

Only then did he turn to Sarah, standing rather quiet and pale beside him.

'Much as I commend your bravery, Sarah, I must beg you never to risk your safety again—I cannot keep an eye on you all the time…'

'Keep an eye on me?' Her voice was rather shrill, what with indignation and delayed fright. 'I haven't seen you for days.'

Mr ter Breukel sighed. 'No, and for several good reasons. The answer is for us to get married.'

'Well, you may if you wish,' snapped Sarah. 'I'll have to wait until someone asks me.'

'If you would just listen, you silly girl. I *am* asking you.'

She looked at him as though he had lost his wits; the drizzle had ceased, there was even a patch or two of blue sky, but the wind was cold and she shivered, as much with the chilliness as the shock of his words.

'You're asking me?'

He was leaning against the door; now he drew her to stand beside him and put an arm around her shoulders.

'Yes, I am, but let me explain.' He paused, before going on carefully, 'It had occurred to me that we

would be happy together as man and wife, but I felt—
still do feel—that you should first have the opportunity of finding your feet away from home. You have
had no chance to do so, have you? You would have
continued to live at home, tied to your mother's every
wish and whim, disliked by and disliking your stepfather, gradually losing heart and becoming resigned.
You see, Sarah, other girls might run away, but you
have too tender a heart. But now you have discovered
independence, and perhaps you want to spread your
wings?'

She found her voice. 'You want to marry me? But
you don't know anything about me, do you? And—
and you don't love me…'

'Have I not said that I believe we could be happy
together? And if you wished to have a career of some
sort I wouldn't stand in your way; you would be free
to follow your own interests.'

She stared into his calm face. He sounded so kind
and so reasonable, as though getting married was a
simple act, shorn of all doubts. And his argument
made sense too. But it wouldn't be simple at all, she
reflected. She loved him, but he hadn't said that he
loved her, and if she married him she had no wish to
be anything other than his wife, behaving like other
wives: being at home when he got home, seeing that
he had nourishing meals and spotless linen, listening
with a sympathetic ear to him after a hard day's work.
And children—she wanted children—and she wanted
him to love her…

She said slowly, 'I've never been asked to marry
anyone before, so I'm not sure what to say.'

He smiled then. 'Then don't say anything. We will go back to the hospital and I'll drive you home. I shan't stay. Think about it as much as you wish, and when you're ready we'll talk again.'

He stopped himself just in time from kissing her, which was a pity, for it would have put an end to their misunderstanding. Instead he took her arm and walked her back through the almost quiet streets. There were a few people standing about, shopkeepers sweeping up broken glass, car owners examining damaged cars, the odd scuffle as police collected up the remnants of the street gangs.

Sarah was far too busy with her thoughts to notice any of these things. She got into the car and sat without speaking until they reached her home.

Mr ter Breukel got out, opened her door and stood beside her on the pavement.

'You said that you haven't seen me, Sarah. But do remember that I am always there.' He rang the door-bell, waited until Mrs Twist opened the door, and then went back to his car.

Sarah watched him drive away. She longed to marry him, but she wouldn't. He had said that they would be happy together, but supposing that he met a woman he loved? What then?

She followed Mrs Twist into the kitchen, and over supper gave her a watered-down version of the evening.

'A blessing that dear man went after you,' said Mrs Twist. 'A pity 'e couldn't stay for 'is supper.'

Sarah remembered then that she hadn't even offered him a cup of coffee. He had said that he couldn't stay, but she could at least have offered something.

She went to bed presently, and lay awake a long time, imagining life as his wife, until she went to sleep, only to wake in the morning knowing that she was going to refuse him.

She must think up some really good reason—a career in something or other—computers. She had been told that once one had mastered them, there were unending opportunities—super jobs, marvellous salaries, meeting important people. She would find out as much as possible about them so that she would sound convincing. And he would be secretly relieved, she felt sure.

She rehearsed several suitable speeches on her way to work on Monday; she must be ready to give him his answer when next they met—perhaps not that day, but certainly before the week was out. Satisfied that she couldn't improve upon them, she worked even harder than usual in her canteen, outwardly cheerful but with a heart grieving for what might have been.

She didn't see Mr ter Breukel that day, nor the next, and when she did see him again her carefully worded speeches went unspoken.

The letter which had come by that morning's post from her mother had for the moment driven all other thoughts out of her head. She had sat down to read it after breakfast, while Mrs Twist went to the shops. She had read it, and then read it again, not quite believing it.

The letter wasn't long, and a good deal of it was taken up with instructions. Mrs Holt wrote to say that they had decided to move to Bournemouth; they liked the town, they had made many friends, and they had seen a delightful house close to the sea. Her stepfather, went on Mrs Holt, intended to more or less retire, so he would need to go to London only very infrequently. The house at Clapham Common was to be sold, and Sarah and Mrs Twist were to remain in it until a buyer had been found, after which they could travel to Bournemouth. There would be no need for Mrs Holt to return for the moment. Sarah could deal with the estate agents and any prospective buyers, and she and Mrs Twist could start to pack away any silver and china not in use, together with her and Mr Holt's clothes.

Sarah, reading the letter yet again, had looked in vain for some comment as to how she and Mrs Twist might feel about it; her mother had taken it for granted that they would be happy to fall in with her plans. And Sarah was to tell Mrs Twist...

She'd decided to wait and tell the housekeeper when she got home that evening; they could discuss it at their leisure. Perhaps Mrs Twist would choose to go to Bournemouth, after all. But her relations and friends were scattered in and around London, so she might not want to. As for her self, Sarah knew that she would never go to Bournemouth.

But perhaps here was the solution to her problem; she could tell Mr ter Breukel that her mother and stepfather were moving from the Clapham Common house and wished her to join them. She would be able to find a job there, she would tell him, and meet any number of people. She wouldn't be telling a lie, she assured herself, just altering the truth a little, and as soon as he had gone back to Holland she would find other work.

It shouldn't be too hard; she would get a reference from the hospital, and she had been saving her wages. Not to marry him would break her heart, but even worse was the thought of marrying a man who didn't love her. Oh, he liked her, they were friends, and he had been unfailingly kind each time they had met, but that was no foundation for a marriage.

She rehearsed a number of now suitable speeches, and then, when they did meet, forgot them all.

They came face to face in the entrance hall, she on her way home, he on the way to check on his patients from his morning list in Theatre. It was no place in which to have a lengthy talk but he stopped in front of her, blocking her path with his bulk.

'Are you going home?' he asked without preamble. 'Because if you are may I come and see you later?'

Sarah said quickly, 'Can you spare five minutes now? I'll be very quick. I've had a letter from my mother. They're selling the house at Clapham Common and have bought one in Bournemouth. They want me to go and live with them there. It's a bit of a surprise, but it's like an answer, isn't it? I mean, I'll be able to start afresh, get a job, meet people.'

Mr ter Breukel's face showed none of his feelings; he said in a level voice, 'That is what you want, Sarah? You believe that this is really your chance to change your life, become independent? You would be happy?'

'Oh, yes,' said Sarah, and prayed for forgiveness

for such a whopping lie. 'So you see there's no need for you to marry me.' She swallowed the lump in her throat. 'Thank you very much for asking me.'

He smiled. It was a bitter smile, but his voice was friendly enough. 'I must be glad that your future has become so promising. I'm sure you will make a success of whatever you choose to do.'

Sarah said, 'Yes, so there's no need for you to come this evening.' She looked up into his expressionless face. 'I wouldn't have liked you to have come all the way to Clapham just to hear that I'd decided to change my mind.'

He agreed gravely. So she *had* intended to marry him, had she? And now she had changed her mind. He wondered why. Something he would find out.

They parted in a friendly fashion, going their separate ways, he to his patients, thrusting all thoughts of her from his mind for the moment, she to stand in a long queue for a bus, longing to get home so that she could go somewhere quiet and cry until she had no tears left.

She saw him two days later, passing him on her way to the basement stairs. He stopped, wished her a friendly good afternoon, and told her that he would be returning to Holland on the following day.

Sarah put out a hand and managed a smile. 'I hope you have a good journey. Will you be in Holland for a long time?'

'Three weeks—a month. Then back here very briefly. You will probably be gone by then.'

'Yes, I suppose so. Please give my love to Suzanne. And thank you for all your kindness.'

There was really nothing more to say. 'I'll be late,' she said, and raced down the stairs. Well, that's over, she told herself, I must get away from here before he comes back. Brave words, drowned in unshed tears.

Mrs Twist, informed of her employers' plans, had refused to go to Bournemouth; her family and friends were scattered around London and that was where she belonged. She'd agreed to stay at home until it was sold.

Mrs Holt had written Sarah another long letter demanding that she went to Bournemouth as quickly as possible so that she might accompany her mother on the shopping expeditions necessary for the new house. She was to pack up the ornaments and silver, and their clothes, and oversee the removal of a good deal of the furniture.

'Two weeks should be ample time for you to see to this,' the letter had said. 'We shall expect you no later than that.'

Mr ter Breukel had gone; Sarah gave in her notice and wrote and told her mother that she would see to the packing up of the things she wished for, and arrange for the furniture to be collected, but that she herself would be staying in London. 'I have a good job and somewhere to live,' she wrote recklessly, 'and I intend to become independent. I am sure that you and my stepfather will be very happy in your new home, but please understand that I would like to lead a life of my own...'

Naturally enough, this letter caused a flood of telephone calls and indignant letters, to which Sarah replied firmly. 'It isn't that I don't love you, Mother, as you suggest, but I do wish for my own life, and you must agree with me that my stepfather will be glad not to have me in the house. Once you are settled in, with a good housekeeper and everything to your liking, I'm sure that you will see the good sense of this. Later on, when I get my holidays, I will come and visit you.'

Mrs Twist, shocked at first at Sarah's decision, agreed that it was a chance which might never occur again. 'Just as long as yer get a good job…'

'Oh, I shall,' said Sarah airily. 'I'll stay here until I do. It may take a week or two until I find something I would like to do.'

Mrs Twist studied her face. 'Let's hope so. You look peaked, Miss Sarah, and you've got thin. That job at the hospital was too hard work.'

It had certainly been that, agreed Sarah silently, but Litrik had been there too. She thought about him constantly, and now she would never see him again she called him Litrik. It didn't matter any more; he had really gone out of her life, and now she had left the canteen there were no more snatches of gossip to be gleaned about him.

She began looking for work, setting about it in a dogged fashion, answering anything which sounded suitable for her meagre talents. But she had no luck; her letters were ignored, or she was told the job had been filled, and the few interviews she went to were unsuccessful. She had so few skills, and serving in a canteen, however good her reference was, wasn't enough.

Finally she found work, filling shelves at a supermarket. It was part-time, from half past seven in the morning until noon, and it was work she could do without needing anything other than an ability to work hard and quickly and to be honest. It was only a short bus ride from her home too, and although the wages weren't much she was able to save almost all of her pay packet since she was still living at home.

But there was a prospective buyer for the house, and she would need to earn more money if she had to find a bedsitter. She became a little thinner, and a little paler, and muddled in with her worries was the constant image of Litrik.

Sarah had been working at the supermarket for a week when Mr ter Breukel returned to London. And, being a man very much in love despite the hopelessness of the situation, he went straight to the hospital; he wanted to be sure that she was still intent on going to Bournemouth. He had no intention of giving up until she actually left London; indeed he had no intention of giving up even then.

He found his way to the Domestic Supervisor's office, exchanged civilities, and enquired if Sarah Beckwith was still working on the same shift.

The supervisor managed not to look surprised. Whatever next? A senior consultant seeking the whereabouts of one of the girls in the canteen? All the same, she answered him readily enough.

'Sarah? She left us, let me see, about three weeks ago. A good worker, too; I was sorry to see her go, sir.'

He thanked her pleasantly and went back to his car, then made the slow journey through the rush-hour traffic to Clapham Common. It was still early morning; if Sarah was at home he would have no compunction in getting her out of her bed. For all he knew she might be on the point of leaving.

The house, when he reached it, looked forlorn, and as he waited for someone to answer his knock he noticed that the downstairs windows lacked curtains. But someone was there; he heard footsteps in the hall and a moment later Mrs Twist opened the door.

'Lor' bless me, sir, and here was me thinking I'd never see you again.'

She stood aside for him to go in and he saw that the hall carpet had been taken up and that there were pale squares on the walls where the pictures had hung.

'Sarah has gone to Bournemouth, Mrs Twist?'

'No, sir, and never meant to. 'Ad a bit of a do with her ma, told 'er she'd got a good job here and meant to stay.' Mrs Twist snorted. 'Good job—she's working part-time at the supermarket in the High Street, filling shelves. Goes in the morning early and finishes at midday. And what she'll do in a week's time when the new owners move in, I don't know.'

Mr ter Breukel frowned. 'She told me she was going to live with her mother and stepfather... Where is this supermarket?'

'Go left at the end of the road and then take the second turning on the right; that'll bring you to it. There's a car park.'

He smiled suddenly. 'We shall be back shortly, Mrs Twist...'

Mrs Twist's nose twitched at the scent of romance. *'We,* sir?'

'Yes, Mrs Twist.'

The supermarket was crowded with shoppers. Mr ter Breukel found an assistant and asked to be taken to the Manager. Presently he found himself in a small crowded office with a harassed-looking man at the desk.

'If I might have a word,' began Mr ter Breukel, assuming what could only be described as his best bedside manner. Ten minutes later they left the office together, threading their way to the back of the place where the manager opened a door and invited him to go in.

'Will you need to see Miss Beckwith again?' asked Mr ter Breukel.

'No, there's no need. This is all very unusual, but in the circumstances…'

They shook hands, and Mr ter Breukel went in and shut the door behind him. Sarah was unpacking tomato soup, stacking the tins on a small trolley. She didn't turn round when she heard the door close.

'This is the last lot, when you're ready.'

She turned round then, and saw him. It was as though someone had lighted her pale face with a soft glow, and he allowed himself a huge sigh of relief.

'Oh,' said Sarah, 'how did you get here? Who told you? Why are you here anyway?'

He said with commendable calm, 'Hello, Sarah. I came in my car. Mrs Twist told me where to find you, and I've come to take you home.'

She said in a shaky voice, 'Well, I can't come yet. It's only half past ten.'

'You've resigned. I have seen the manager; you're free to leave now.'

Her mouth fell open. 'Resigned? But I've only been here a week, and I need a job.'

'No, you don't. But let us not stand here arguing. If you will get your coat I'll drive you back, then we can talk.'

'What about?'

'Us.'

She could see that there would be no arguing about it. Meekly she took off her overall, found her coat and went with him to his car. They drove the short distance without saying a word. Sarah felt as though she had been hit on the head and had become delirious, while he was perfectly calm and relaxed.

Mrs Twist made coffee and they sat in the kitchen, the only room in the house that still held any comfort. Mr ter Breukel ate all the biscuits, since he had missed his breakfast, and listened sympathetically to Mrs Twist's problems until Sarah, unable to sit there any longer wondering what was to happen next, murmured something about packing the china. All nonsense, of course, but it got her out of the room.

Mr ter Breukel paused long enough to thank Mrs Twist for his coffee and went after her, to find her in the dining room at the back of the house, which was now quite empty, smelling slightly of damp and emptiness. He shut the door after him and crossed the bare boards, and turned her round to face him.

'Before we say anything else, let us get one thing

quite clear. I love you, Sarah, and I want to marry
you. And if you would just throw your odd notions
out of the window and learn to love me a little, I
believe that we will be extremely happy together.'

He put his arms around her and pulled her close.
'I fell in love with you when I saw you first. I've told
you that, but I'll tell you again…'

'You didn't tell me that you loved me.'

'No, I wanted you to be free to choose.' He kissed
the top of her head. 'You told me that you were going
to Bournemouth, and I thought you had chosen.'

'I didn't know you loved me, did I? Oh, Litrik, I
love you too, only I've been so silly.'

'My darling girl, never that. At cross purposes, perhaps.' He wrapped her even closer and began to kiss
her…

Presently, Sarah asked, 'How long will you be here
in London?'

'A week only. You can stay here? No, that's un-
thinkable.' He thought for a moment, then kissed her
once more. 'I have it. I have a little house in a village
in Somerset; you shall go there, and Mrs Twist shall
go with you if she would like that. We can be married
there—the church is small and beautiful. I'll ask
Suzanne to come over and keep you company. I'll
have to go back to Arnhem for a couple of days, but
I'll get a special licence and we'll marry the moment
I come back.'

Sarah said, 'I haven't anything to wear.'

'That's easily dealt with. Am I going too fast for
you, my dearest?'

'Yes, but I rather like it.' She stretched up to kiss

him, to lend weight to her words. 'Of course there are all kinds of problems. Mother…?'

'We'll drive down and tell her. I'm free on Sunday.'

'She'll be angry.'

'I'll be with you, darling.'

They went out to lunch then, taking Mrs Twist with them, who was thrilled to bits at the idea of the wedding and equally delighted to go with Sarah to Somerset.

By the end of the meal Litrik had everything arranged. He would take her and Mrs Twist straight from Bournemouth to his country home, they would see the rector, and there would be no need for Sarah to return to London. And as for Mrs Twist, she had no doubt that she could get a nephew to mind the house while she was away. He left after lunch, and Sarah went back to the house with Mrs Twist and sat in the kitchen, wrapped in dreams.

It all went exactly as planned. Her mother had been angry, and then peevish, and Sarah, with Litrik beside her, had listened a little sadly, for it was apparent that her mother regarded her as an unpaid companion who would have to be replaced. Whatever Litrik had had to say to her stepfather had been brief. He'd refused to come to their wedding, but when Litrik had suggested that he would send a car to take her mother to ceremony, she'd agreed to go. 'I hope it's a decent affair,' she'd said, 'and not some hole-and-corner ceremony.'

They had left then, and driven up to Somerset to

the small village where Litrik had his house. A nice, solid old house, not too large, with a lovely garden and open country at its back. He had a housekeeper there, a widow lady who lived in the village. She had opened the door to them with a warm smile, and a moment later a door had opened and Suzanne had rushed to meet them.

'I'm here until the wedding. It's Litrik's idea; I hope you're glad. We're going shopping…'

Litrik had left them then, and driven back to London. That evening he'd made a number of phone calls. After all, what were old friends for? Everything had gone according to plan. The rector had been helpful, the business of getting the licence was well in hand.

Litrik slept the sleep of a contented man, emptied his head of everything but his work each day, and only each evening did he phone Sarah.

Sarah got up early on her wedding day, and went to look out of the window. It was going to be good weather: blue sky and warm sunshine. And Litrik would be coming. The week had been restful and pleasant, for Suzanne was a good companion. They had shopped, and Suzanne had insisted on buying a white dress and a little veil. It was a very simple dress, but it suited her, and presently she went to her room to put it on. She was still in her dressing gown when Litrik knocked and came in.

He caught her close and kissed her. 'Mrs Twist is shocked. I'm not supposed to see you until we meet at church.' He took two cases from a pocket. 'There has been no time. We'll have to be engaged for an hour or so.' He slipped a sapphire and diamond ring on her finger and then opened the other case, saying, 'Pearls for my bride.'

He saw the tears in her eyes. 'My darling, don't cry.'

'I'm not. I'm just so happy.' She smiled then. 'Litrik, I don't know anything—will someone give me away? And where are we going afterwards, or may we stay here? And will the church be empty?'

He stooped to kiss her once more. 'Dr Benson is giving you away.'

He had gone again before she could ask any more questions. 'It's all topsy-turvy,' she told her reflection in the mirror as she arranged her veil just so. 'The bride's mother usually does everything and the bridegroom just turns up.'

Presently she found herself in the church porch, a bouquet of white roses in her hand and Dr Benson beside her. When they entered the church it wasn't empty at all. There was her mother, in a magnificent hat, there was Mrs Twist and Litrik's housekeeper, and there was Suzanne and the nice Professor Smythe. There were others too, friends of Litrik, she supposed, and people from the village.

She was suddenly so happy that she wanted to sing and dance, only of course she couldn't, not in this beautiful little church, with the organ playing softly and the rector waiting to marry them. And Litrik, dear Litrik, turning to look at her as she reached his side, a look so full of love that she caught her breath.

The rector began, 'Dearly beloved...' And Sarah

thought, Oh, how exactly right, and slipped her hand into Litrik's. She felt his firm clasp, knowing that his hand would always be there when she needed it. She looked at the rector then, and he saw that she, whom he had thought of as a rather plain girl, was beautiful.

Modern Romance™
...seduction and
passion guaranteed

Tender Romance™
...love affairs that
last a lifetime

Sensual Romance™
...sassy, sexy and
seductive

Blaze™
...sultry days and
steamy nights

Medical Romance™
...medical drama on
the pulse

Historical Romance™
...rich, vivid and
passionate

29 new titles every month.

*With all kinds of Romance for
every kind of mood...*

MILLS & BOON®

Makes any time special™

MAT

The perfect gift this Christmas from

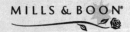

MILLS & BOON®

3 brand new romance novels and a FREE French manicure set

for just £7.99

featuring best selling authors
Betty Neels,
Kim Lawrence and Nicola Cornick

Available from 19th October

0801/123/MB19

OTHER NOVELS BY

PENNY JORDAN

MILLS & BOON®

MILLS & BOON
FOREIGN AFFAIRS
A captivating 12 book collection of sun-kissed seductions.
Enjoy romance around the world
DON'T MISS BOOK 2
french kiss–
Proposals Parisian style
Available from 2nd November
Available at most branches of WH Smith, Tesco, Martins, Borders, Eason, Sainsbury's, and most good paperback bookshops.
FA/RTL/2